# THE TAÀR

## **DYSTOPIA** BOOK ONE

# THE TAÀR

## **DYSTOPIA** BOOK ONE

To Ben,
Bonello
2021

John A. Bonello

SERAFIN™
BOOKS

A Serafin Books publication



Website: www.johnabonello.com
Email: johnabonello@gmail.com



This book is a work of fiction. Names, characters, businesses, organizations, places and events are either the product of the author's imagination or are used fictitiously. Any resemblance to actual persons, events or locales is entirely coincidental.

Cover illustration by Derek Fenech
http://derekfenech.com/

ISBN: 978-99957-1-140-5
ISBN eBook: 978-99957-1-141-2

# DEDICATION

To Duncan. A friend. A brother.

*Futility is the defining characteristic of life. Pain is proof of existence.*

Stephen R. Donaldson

Lord Foul's Bane (The Chronicles of Thomas Covenant the Unbeliever, #1)

What you're about to read took place in a distant future. It happened also in a distant past, and is probably taking place right now. Such is the nature of humanity.

# PROLOGUE – THE LAST GIRL IN THE TOWER

Ela woke up with a fright. Without thinking, she moved her hands to her big round belly, ensuring it was still there. She wondered what had woken her up.

A flash of light filled the room for just a second. The darkness returned, stronger, complete. Propping herself up on her elbows, Ela looked out of the window to her left. A silent lightning storm was raging outside, the noise completely sealed out by the thick glass. The sky flashed again. For a moment she saw rain drops dotting the glass.

A heartbeat later she felt it. The pain was slight at first, a nuisance. Then it grew stronger and stronger with each breath, until she was certain it was what had disturbed her sleep–a burning pain in her lower back. It was gone as fast as it came. Relieved, she felt a movement inside her and smiled like she did every time she felt those little kicks from within. But the smile was wiped off her face when the pain returned once more, this time stronger than before. A loud, long moan escaped her lips.

Panic overcame her, as she became suddenly aware of what was happening. Tiny cold beads of sweat sprouted on her forehead. *How is this possible*, she thought. *Why so early?* The due date was still nearly ten weeks away.

Without getting up, she put out her left hand and touched a part of the wall behind the bedside table. A warm yellowish glow filled the room. It was dim at first, then gradually got stronger. She sat up, slowly. The pain returned and almost made her bend double. She told herself to calm down, but could not.

Her hands found and pressed a button protruding from the wall, beneath the light switch. After a few moments the room's door slid open with a low *swooshing* noise, like two pieces of cloth rubbing against each other. A young man walked in–Kari, one of the nursing staff on night duty.

Smiling, he asked her if she needed anything. During the past five months she had often called him during the night for a glass of cold water or sometimes just to chat a little when she couldn't sleep. He was a gentle soul and she liked his company.

As soon as he saw her face contort under yet another bout of pain, his smile faded and was replaced by worry. He ran to her side.

Grabbing his left arm she implored him to call Lor, to hurry up, as the baby was coming. Kari didn't understand straight away. He asked if she might be mistaken. It was still early. Ela assured him she knew what she was saying. She was certain. Again, she asked him to call the doctor, her voice brusque, out of breath.

It seemed like ages later when the young nurse reappeared through the door followed by an ageing physician. Lor did not ask any questions. He walked right up to the bed and started feeling Ela's belly with his warm hands, putting pressure in certain areas to ensure the baby's position within the womb. He asked her to lie back down and prop up her legs, so he could examine her better. It took him only a minute, after which he turned on Kari and asked him to go wake up everyone, then head to the delivery room and make it ready, urging him to make haste. The baby was going to be with them soon.

Kari left. The old physician looked at the girl and smiled.

No need to worry, he told her kindly. Gently, he brushed her hair away from her face, telling her everything was going to be fine. Lor joked, saying this was happening because her baby was fed up inside her and wanted to get out in the light. Had she thought of a name yet?

She laughed nervously. No, she had not. She knew it had to happen, only not this early. She had assumed her child would be born when due.

When months before they had asked her if she would be willing to help in ensuring the survival of their race, she accepted without hesitation, despite her fears. She knew the day would come when they would ask, had been expecting it from when she was old enough to understand how humans reproduced. They wanted her to be the mother of the new generation of tower people, denizens of a most peculiar future. She was young, and knew it. But the doctors encouraged her and assured her repeatedly that her body was ready to bear her children. And her children were destined to be the future of humanity.

Ela was the last girl in the tower, the last glimpse of hope in a world where all hope was lost forever. Harvested by the cruel scythe of nuclear war.

This was her moment of truth. Fear welled up inside her, strong and threatening and she knew Lor was seeing it through her eyes. They moved her to another room on the same floor, a colder room, without any windows, full of strange blinking equipment, tools and strong medicinal odours.

The pain was now nailing her down to the bed and she cried out shamelessly every time the contractions came. The physician was examining her again and saying something to another doctor.

Hold still, he told her. Bear the pain a little longer. It will soon be over. He said this in a low soothing monotone, explaining why he could not give her anything to alleviate the pain. It was too late, and they did not want to risk harming the baby. She would have to give birth the traditional way, as was done in the distant past. Holding her cold hands in his, he told her again to take heart. A woman's body was made to bear children, and the pain was part of the process that helped the birth.

Empty words. She was but a girl. And after all, it was *she* who felt the pain and no one else. Thoughts raced in her head, chiefly among them a question. *Why did I ever agree to this?*

More medical staff came in, wearing masks, surgical gloves and long white robes. They went busily around their tasks, mechanical in their movements, concentrating, silent. She knew each and every one of them, but with their masks covering their mouths and the caps on their heads they seemed like total strangers. Lor told her to do as told, to have faith in them. Everything was going to be all right, he repeated.

But Ela's mind was elsewhere, locked up in a world of her own, made of pain and suffering. Nothing else mattered. She felt nothing, was aware of nothing. Nothing but her pain. The people moving around her were like noise. She never heard them urging her to take deep breaths, neither to wait and push only when told.

She couldn't take it any longer, could not wait. She felt the need to push with all her might, and push is what she did. She pushed and pushed, trying to drive the pain away.

And at last she felt herself being emptied. A sense of loss as something drifted out of her. She heard cries, but they were already distant. She felt light as a feather, moving away, soaring, soaring higher, eyes closing in a peaceful dreamless sleep that engulfed her entirely.

Ela, the last girl, the last mother, gave birth to a boy. Just one child. Then it was over. She closed her eyes forever.

# Part One

# The Desolation

# 1 UNDER THE RUBBLE

The large concrete block he had been trying to dislodge, finally gave way, exposing what lay underneath. It tumbled down the side of the rubble heap upon which he was working. Echoes of the crash resounded all around before gradually dying out. A massive cloud of dust rose up, quickly dispersing in the strong south easterly wind.

He straightened up, his chest heaving with the effort, and for a few moments looked around, first to his immediate vicinity, then letting his gaze drift farther away. The height of the mound where he stood gave him a good vantage point. Nothing had changed. No movement could be detected as far as his eyes could see. From the indistinguishable mounds of rubble that were once buildings, to the familiar gleaming tower in the distance and beyond, all was still.

Behind his protective mask, dark bird-like eyes moved up to the reddish sky, completely overcast with dust clouds. The sun, permanently hidden by that heavy crimson blanket, would soon go down in the west. Only a couple of hours remained in which to find something of value. His mates, working in pairs on similar mounds in that same zone, had not been luckier than him so far.

Bending back to his work, the boy squeezed through the irregular shaped hole exposed by the block. But once more, any hope of finding something was crushed when he realized the way down was blocked by more rubble. He climbed back out immediately, moved to another part of the heap, and started all over again. Rocks and debris tumbled down the heap as he carefully searched for a way in. He made an effort to keep focused on the rocks he removed. If he dislodged one that held other boulders in place he would end up crushed or worse. It wasn't the first time the rubble had caved-in underneath him, as had happened so many times to other scavengers, including long lost friends and relatives. He had been lucky so far, although his body was covered with scars and bruises as a reminder of the ever present peril.

He worked as fast as he could, glancing up every now and again to ensure there wasn't any danger. Cold wasn't the only thing that followed darkness in that place. The devil-dogs hunted in packs and the closer it got to sunset the greater the risk of encounter.

Removing the mask–a breathing apparatus without which he would end up inhaling only sand and dust–the boy wiped sweat and grime from his brow with the back of his hand. He wore the mask all the time when he was out scavenging. They had plenty of them back at the temple, but he was one of the few who wore them. Others preferred using a common piece of cloth to cover their noses and mouths.

The boy replaced the mask and went on working. He had already gone back empty handed the day before, and if he went back today and told the Taàr he hadn't found anything, the old man would burst out in anger and probably beat him to a pulp.

He removed a narrow but long piece of concrete, than another. As soon as he touched a stone the length of his arm, a section of loose dirt and rubble collapsed inwardly, revealing a new hole, wide enough for his head to go through. He fished out a little torch light out of a large pouch sewn at the back of his trousers, and switched it on into the hole. *At last*, he thought.

Through the hole he saw a room–a square space, once part of a house that like every other building in that desolate place was swept away in the blink of an eye. Doomsday. That's how those who survived the day referred to the massive atomic strike that changed the Earth forever. He had seen hundreds of similar rooms, most of which led to plentiful loots–things of value to the Taàr's people. Some led to nothing, so he didn't build his hopes up too high. Not just yet.

He widened the hole slightly, enough to squeeze through–he was pitifully thin, like others his age. He had just turned fourteen and had been out scavenging the zones since he was six. At first just gathering wood and other fuel for fire, later assisting older boys when looking for food or water. Kids in his clan had to start helping out from an early age. There was no other way.

Just two years before he and his brother had been inseparable. They scavenged together until the day Rorik ended up buried alive inside a building that collapsed just as he was coming out with the last load. From that day on, the boy never wanted anyone with him, choosing to work alone. The Taàr disapproved of this, and said so many times, but until now had never taken any action. The rest of the Younglings, as their band called themselves, silently accepted the boy's decision and left him alone most of the time.

Rorik had been ten years his senior, a skilled scavenger, never one to take uncalculated risks. Maybe that was the reason why the younger brother could not accept his death. Or maybe it was because he had been the only family he had left–other than their Uncle Sam, but he considered him a stranger more than anyone else. Rorik had been the only living soul who could tell him about his mother and father whenever he felt like hearing stories about them. Both parents died when he was just a year old. He and Rorik had been the only two children to survive out of eight siblings.

His brother had often recalled the cruel fate that befell the other six. Three had been still-born, two were born severely malformed and lived only a few months, and another one lived to three years, then got sick and died in a matter of days. Everyday incidents for the people of Tartarys. The toxic radioactive environment made for difficult living conditions. It made for a hard, ruthless life.

He thought of his brother as he went down through the hole. In moments like those, Rorik used to take a large breath, hold up two crossed fingers and make a wish. *Let's hope we find our share today.* He imagined him there, beside him, saying those words in his gruff voice. The boy murmured those words. Maybe it was a way to keep the tradition alive. Or maybe to keep his brother alive.

The hint of a smile had appeared on the boy's lips as soon as Rorik's memory welled up inside him. But now the smile wore off as he focused on the new dim surroundings.

The room he had lowered himself into had once been a bedroom. Someone, more than seventy years in the past, had lived in that luxury. Someone was lucky enough to have a room for themselves, with a bed and matching furniture now rotting, with a small desk still covered with pencils and pens and three shelves full of books that were now only ash. Everything turned to ash, eventually.

The boy could only imagine the room as it had once been. He had never experienced any of that sort. All he knew was hardship and suffering, a life of darkness. And ash.

Moving to a corner of the room, he went through an open doorway into a short corridor filled with bits of concrete that had fallen from the ceiling. There was enough space for the boy to crawl through to the end, until he came to a stairs that went down into complete darkness. He projected the small light in front of him and descended carefully, as quiet as a mouse. Now that he had gone below, the noise of the wind had completely subsided and the silence was total. He could hear his breathing through the protective mask, his footsteps on the ash covered tiles, and he thought he could even make out his heart beating fast in his chest.

The stairs led down to a floor with two more bedrooms, a bathroom and a large kitchen. He went into the latter, shaking the torch every few minutes to recharge it. The tiny light silently revealed the contents of the room. First to be exposed was the table, where the remains of a human being lay. The person had probably been seated at the table when death walked into that kitchen. The skeleton was still intact from the hips up, with the arms and head resting on the glass surface, while the rest of the body lay in a heap of dust under the table. He had found similar scenes during their scavenges, and he could never understand why some skeletons remained intact while others became dust. Rorik's theory was that it all depended on what the persons ate during their lifetime. The boy walked beside the skeleton and touched the head. He wanted to check if it was in good condition so he could take it to Pat, who collected skulls. But it disintegrated as soon as his fingers touched the yellowed bone. Only the teeth remained, shining in the torchlight.

The boy turned his light on the rest of the kitchen. He spotted some utensils still in the sink, hanging cupboards that had long since crashed down, china plates and bowls scattered across the floor, some broken, some intact. He was not interested in these artefacts–they had thousands of similar items in their stores. What he picked up was a small earthenware saucer, decorated with tiny red flowers. This he pocketed before continuing the search for food or drink.

Opening one of the bottom cupboard doors, he found dozens of cans of food. The wrapper around the cans was yellowish, crumbling, but the cans looked in good condition.

He picked one up, shook it, and with satisfaction heard a slosh inside. He suddenly relaxed, feeling the tension within him dissipate into tiredness.

His stomach grumbled with hunger. It

pleaded him to open one can and feed himself. He hadn't eaten since the day before. All he had taken since that morning was a glass of water. But he quickly abolished the thought. Vivid memories of what had happened when he once dared open a can of food came rushing back to him–the thousands, if not millions, of roaches and rats that surrounded them when he had not even finished eating the whole can, then the furious devil-dogs that ran after him and his brother, perhaps more because they had heard their screams than because they smelled the food. And after all that mess, the beating they got from Sal.

Shuddering at these thoughts, he opened more cupboards and found more canned food, as well as bottled drinks. Sometimes liquids would be too rancid for consumption, but more often than not, they would find acceptable ones.

From the same pocket where he kept the torch and other tools, he took out four carefully folded empty canvas sacks and started filling them with cans. He didn't have enough space to carry out all the loot. When the sacks were full enough, he climbed back upstairs with the first two, went back through the corridor, and left the goods in the bedroom. Then he squeezed outside and fished a piece of red cloth from the usual pocket.

Looking around, he found a suitable jagged piece of concrete on which to tie the cloth that served as a marker. When he finished tying, he took off the mask, put two fingers in his mouth, and whistled loudly. It was a call old Sal had thought them to communicate over long distances.

He repeated the same sound three times–a signal indicating he had found something to take home–then replaced the mask and went back inside. It was good to be out of the wind. He went back down and carried the remaining sacks up.

To while away the time, he rummaged

through the wardrobe. The clothes inside became dust as soon as he laid fingers on them. At the bottom he found a couple of rotten boxes filled with shoes that had become too hard to be of any use.

The first reply camc, ending his search. His companions had heard his call and were grouping up to his location. One long whistle meant they were asking him for directions–with the strong wind blowing at all times, it was difficult to determine where a whistle came from. He went back to the hole in the ceiling, stuck out his head, lifted the mask and whistled three more times. After a little while, his friends appeared.

## 2 SUFFERING

It was almost dark when the boy and his mates finally made it to their abode–a huge construction, built on the crest of a hill, surrounded by the remains of the small town of Tartarys. A town shrouded in silence. Three enormous doors set in an imposing façade barred the way into the building.

Many years before, the current Taàr and his less than four hundred followers found shelter in that building and made it their home. Before that time, under previous Taàrs, the clan had roamed the zones like nomads, never settling in the same place for a long time. They would stay just enough to scavenge an area, then move on to the next. The people lived in constant fear of attacks from a rival clan and so chose to keep moving to avoid being easily located.

But when Sal became Taàr, he led his people to the town of Tartarys, back to where he was born. He knew the town and the temple, knew that once cleared and cleaned it would make a stronghold for them, with enough space for everyone. He did so partly because of the clan's dwindling numbers–he argued that roaming like they did without ever settling down was causing the decline in their ranks and soon they would become too few to sustain themselves. The other reason was that they needed a central place from where they could organise searches, increase efficiency, store supplies and ensure some kind of future. They needed somewhere to call *home.* Apart from this, the building was strong and easy to defend against their enemies.

Sal had been proven right. Since settling

in, the clan had grown to four hundred and fifty people. Men, women and children led by a wrinkled old white-bearded man with one good eye and another he kept covered at all times. At seventy five years of age, Sal was the only living man to remember life before doomsday. When in the mood, he often told tales of better days when that same building was a centre of activity in Tartarys, visited by many who prayed and worshipped long forgotten gods. The gods who had forgotten *them*.

From that place, the Taàr's clan controlled their territory, an area that extended to half the island. The other half belonged to the Baron and his people, feared rivals and enemies of the Taàr's clan. The border between the two territories was marked by the only building in that land to withstand the bombing and its aftermath–a gleaming white tower by day, a blue beacon by night. Reaching up past the clouds, with a perimeter as wide as a whole city, the scavenger clans used it as a landmark. Its proper name was the Nimbus Tower, a remnant of another age. But no one used that name. Everyone called it simply *the tower.* And every single one of them knew what the tower represented–Sal made sure of that. By the passing of time, its purpose and function became mysterious to the scavengers, almost mythological. A mysterious landmark they had never been able to unlock.

According to Sal, the tower belonged to the people responsible for the cruel destiny that befell the world, the remorseless murderers of whole populations, of families, of children and parents, old and young. Those monsters built a tower able to withstand almost anything, then they unleashed doom over the entire world. He drummed this knowledge into every member of his clan. He reminded them of what the tower stood for every single night, forbidding anyone to even go near that building. In recent years, many had seen strange beings near the tower, and after those sightings began, Sal warned his people to steer clear should they ever encounter people from that place. Hide, he used to tell them, hide and do not move until they're gone.

Out of Sal's earshot, some had it that the inhabitants of the tower had long since perished. However, others whispered that the sightings were real–someone or other had seen the strange slow moving people themselves. Some said they were tall as giants, some said those wandering through the broken roads and shattered remains of towns and villages were the ghosts of the original tenants of the Nimbus Tower. Still, everyone kept clear of the place.

Alex, one of their band, was waiting for them beside two women standing guard on either side of the temple's middle door. The women looked at them sourly as they went in with the loot. No one enjoyed staying outside the doors after the sun had set. As a rule, the doors opened every morning at dawn and closed at twilight. Those who did not return by sundown had to find their own shelter.

There were valid reasons for that curfew. Once the devil-dogs caught the scent of humans, they stopped at nothing to sink their teeth in their flesh. Too many lives had been lost to the beasts' night raids.

For many, it was difficult to believe that the fearsome dogs were once timid and friendly creatures kept by humans as pets within their homes.

The wild creatures now prowled the night, hunting in packs for rat or man alike.

When the Younglings saw they wouldn't make it in time, they had sent Alex back to the temple before them to let the women on guard know they were coming.

Immediately beyond the magnificent doors lay a roofless area. The roof had caved in long ago. After clearing the rubble, Sal and his people had built a second wall there and fitted it with a metal door. This served as additional protection and also to enclose the inner temple whose roof was still mostly intact, held by two rows of massive limestone pillars. The space inside was cavernous, the ceiling so high that the light of burning candles didn't reach it. The boy spent hours staring at that ceiling, wondering at the skill and knowledge their ancestors must have held in order to build something so colossal.

Beyond the pillars, on either side of temple, rows of mattresses had been laid out side by side and made up the sleeping quarters of the clan. Sal was the only one who didn't sleep there. He shared a room at the back of the temple with Kim, his lifelong partner. She was a kind and wise old woman, some years younger than Sal. Loved by everyone in the clan, she took care of things the Taàr didn't have the disposition to handle. The people respected them both, and many were awed by their longevity in an age where very few reached fifty.

The wide space in the middle, between

the colonnades, held long wooden tables upon which all members of the clan were now seated, eating their only meal of the day. High above them, the roof arced majestically until it reached its highest point. There, through a partly collapsed cupola, light filtered in during the day to wash the interior in a dull red hue.

A hush fell over the place as everyone stopped talking while the band of nine boys approached. Seven sacks full of canned food and bottles were dropped to the floor with a metallic thump and the nine moved to join their brethren to eat.

But the Taàr's dry voice stopped them dead in their tracks. He wanted to know where they had been and the reason for being late. He asked this gruffly, without ever lifting his face out of the food tin from which he was eating.

They remained standing, all of them. To Sal's left, as usual, sat Sam, the boy's uncle, looking at them menacingly. The resemblance to his nephew was remarkable. They shared the same dark complexion, similar small dark eyes and a flat nose with very thin lips. He had a dark beard which the boy did not yet possess, and his head was completely bald, unlike the boy who had long hair that went down to his neckline. Despite this resemblance however, there was little else that uncle and nephew had in common. After Rorik passed away, Sam barely even spoke to the boy.

Sal's question was answered by Edgar, oldest among them. He told him that they had found a good place late in the day and it took them some time to get everything out. Sam made a mocking noise with his mouth, but the Taàr ignored him. He continued eating in silence for a while. Everyone else had stopped eating, and the only sound they could hear was his chewing. When he finished, he slowly wiped his mouth to remove the food from his beard and asked Kim to bring out food for the boys. He told her to give them double ration.

Talking resumed as the Younglings sat down and Kim got up. She called some helpers, then went towards a room at the back, across the marble floor and through a small green door on the right. Back there they kept a store of scavenged food and drinks. Trays laden with stacked bowls and two cans of food for each one of them were brought out and placed on the table together with nine glasses of water.

The boys plunged in, grabbing two cans each, one with mixed vegetables and one with corned beef. They emptied these in their bowls, and started eating immediately. After so many hours working and walking the long distances they were truly famished. Double ration occurred on very rare occasions–Sal allowed it only to reward a good find or an exceptional feat–so they made the most of it. Water was rationed as well. Everyone got three glasses a day, one in the morning, one at midday, and one with dinner. There was no other way to feed everyone.

Seventy one years had gone by since the nuclear bombings had erased villages, cities and whole countries. Those who didn't die instantly were killed later by the effects of the radiation from the fallout which poisoned also trees and vegctation, water, crops, birds, fish and cattle and almost every living thing on the planet. Life trudged on in a rotting, decaying limp, while species dwindled and death celebrated the greatest victory.

Humans numbered but a few, on a sick planet that was quickly turning into a deserted effigy. Fields had been turned to ash. Nothing would grow in the dead soil. The only food they could live on had to be reaped from cans and tins buried beneath the rubble and remains of houses that fell as if made of paper. Collected rain water was contaminated, and so were fresh springs that soon stopped flowing. Many died after drinking from poisoned sources. Sometimes, they found bottled water, sometimes hidden reservoirs that contained water good enough to drink.

They had nothing to test it with but their own mortality. And if it wasn't poisoned water, it was some sickness that took away lives. If not those, then the rabid dogs, that numbered more than the surviving people.

While eating, the boy glanced at Sal and Kim. He pondered, not for the first time, what was special about the couple, how they managed to survive for so long in such a cruel environment. Why didn't his parents enjoy the same fate? And Rorik. *Why did you leave me alone*, thought the boy, still looking at the old couple. Then he felt someone's gaze and his eyes met his uncle's hateful stare. He had grown accustomed to it. It didn't bother him any longer. He turned his head, focused on his food, and ate silently, still wondering about the Taàr and his wife.

Sal was five years old the day the bombs fell. He always said he didn't remember much of that day, but what memories he recalled were not happy ones. The few people who survived that dark day in human history raised

Sal and other children as best they could. They continued their education, despite the circumstances, and ensured some of the knowledge of their ancestors was passed on through them and their children to the next generations. And Sal did try. Some of the older members of the clan were able to read and write. They had learned things about the world of before. But the younger generation showed no interest in learning. Many argued that reading or writing weren't going to help them find food and survive. Books after all, were not good for eating.

Sal never argued back, at least not on that matter.

The Taàr was an able storyteller, perhaps aided by the fact that he alone among his people had lived in a past that had long since ceased to exist. And the sad truth was that if it wasn't for the few books and photographs they sometimes encountered during their forays inside the abandoned houses, no one would have believed some of the tales he told.

A few times every month, after dark, when everyone had finished eating, Sal would gather people around him in a big circle under the broken dome. There he would sit in a chair, and by the light of a candle or one of those artificial lights they sometimes salvaged from the zones, he would read from one of the books he kept in his room. His voice would echo around the silent building, carrying stories from another world. Other times, instead of reading, he would tell them about what he remembered from the time before doomsday and of the days that followed when most of them had not yet been born.

Very few of his tales were happy–they were mostly tragic ones, of great sadness and sorrow that left the listeners heartbroken. There was one tale he liked to repeat often, that of the day he saw the face of death. His descriptions of the people he saw dead or dying, the trees aflame, everything collapsing under a wave of death stirred a heart wrenching grief in those who listened. On that day, some said the Taàr lost his eye, but that was one tale he never told anyone.

After doomsday came famine and pestilence, thousands of decomposing bodies of humans and beasts, death under so many forms and disguises.

And every time Sal recalled how his parents died within months of each other about a year and half after the bombing, the boy would feel himself suffocating under an immense pain. After all, he was an orphan as well, and although his parents died much later, it was still death attributed to the nuclear attack. He couldn't even remember his mother or father's faces. The people of the old world had taken even that memory from him.

Then, at the end of his tale, Sal would silently look those around him in the eye, with a one-eyed stare as hard as Arctic ice that now existed only in photographs and legends. He would reach beneath his shirt to reveal a heavy golden chain that he wore at all times. Raising it high, Sal would show them a little golden cross attached to the chain, upon which the figure of a bleeding man lay nailed. Only suffering could protect them, he would preach, the same pain and suffering worshipped by the people who built the temple hundreds of years in the past. He did not believe in god. No god would have allowed that future to exist. But he did think their ancestors were right to worship suffering. According to Sal, wealth, happiness, global eternal peace, were just illusions, concepts that could never exist without much suffering and sacrifice. And in that suffering they could find themselves, find who they really were.

Only with pain life made sense . . .

# 3 THE QUAIL CALL

Darkness gave way to a harsh first light of dawn. The temple doors came open once more to let out the scavenging bands on their way back to the zones.

The boy walked out with his eight companions, heading east, towards the same area they had been working in for the past weeks. When Rorik was still alive he used to be the leader of the Younglings, a name they gave to themselves for being one of the youngest groups of their clan. After Rorik died, Edgar replaced him as leader but no new member joined their ranks.

The boy never talked much, less so early in the morning, so he kept to himself and started counting his own steps. It was a trick Rorik had thought him to make the road seem a little less long. It was also a way to distract himself, to ensure his mind didn't start pondering his misfortunes. If he stopped counting he would seep instantly into a darkness that mirrored the emptiness and absence of life around him.

Behind him, his friends were laughing, picking on each other, teasing one another. Sometimes he envied their ability to find happiness in all their strife. How did they do it? He was the youngest of the younglings, but sometimes it seemed to him that he alone understood the seriousness of life, as if the others did not see the death, the destruction, the sadness around them.

He didn't want to be drawn in by the darkness of those thoughts. He did not want to contemplate alternatives. But he had stopped counting, and did not resume. So instead, he visualised the great map that Sal had pinned to a wall in the temple. It was made of a thick material, like plastic but tougher, that preserved it well. Rorik used to say that the map had been originally found by their father when he was still very young. Day after day, the old Taàr updated the map with little tin flags cut out from used food cans. Blue marked the spots where food was found, red where searches were fruitless.

With the exception of the house he found the day before and a handful of others, the area they had been assigned was not yet marked. He couldn't predict how things would end up, but right then he felt positive that the area had potential.

After a walk of about an hour and a half under the scorching heat of a hidden sun, they found themselves looking at the red flag the boy had tied the day before. They dispersed in pairs, the boy alone, and resumed the search among the silent mounds, with the wind blowing ceaselessly around them.

Time went by with the usual slowness, and it was past noon when the boy heard the call–the same one he had made the day before. Three whistles. His friends had found something. He lifted his head out of the rubble, dusted himself off, and started in a westerly direction. After a hundred paces or so he stopped. Taking off his mask, he whistled once for directions and waited until a second call resounded. He counted a further sixty paces and then a third call came that left him no doubt of his destination. He found a mound, higher than others around it, and started going around it.

When he was half way round he heard shouting. Angry voices throwing insults, which he immediately recognized as his friends' voices. Then a lower, older voice, calming them down. He did not know that voice. Fear gripped him. Treaty or no treaty, the Baron's people were remorseless savages. He advanced more slowly, careful not to make any noise. His heart started beating faster.

On the other side of the mound he found his friends huddled together with their backs to a tall section of wall that was still intact. A few paces in front of them stood two strangely dressed people. They wore grey suits that made them looked puffed up. Their head was covered by a round glass helmet, while thick long gloves covered their hands. Strange looking boots were on their feet.

Panic had taken hold of his friends. He could see it in their faces, in the movements their hands made as they waved large stones and threw insults at the two men. If they moved another inch, they were saying, they would kill them and throw their bodies to the dogs. The taller of the two grey men replied, his voice calm, his gestures soothing. His words drifted clearly on the wind. The boy understood they had heard the call and moved toward them to meet them.

They should all calm down, he said. He called them friends and went on telling them they needn't worry so much–they came in peace, him and his friend. He promised no one wanted to hurt them. The boy was not sure he heard correctly. The man had said they came from the tower, and that their only wish was to be of help.

Dalin had heard enough. He shouted back that the Taàr's clan needed nobody's help. Go back where you came from, he told them, go back where you belong, go to hell.

But the men from the tower kept their positions. And then the one who had spoken made a step forward–a step he should never have made. Suddenly Dalin and Pat, Jim, Edgar and the other three were upon them, fists and stones flying, feet kicking, and the tower people fell to the ground trying to protect themselves. They offered no resistance, but the boys still hit them until they barely moved.

When it was over, the boy stepped forward. The fight had taken only a matter of seconds. His friends didn't notice him, lost as they were in an adrenalin frenzy, breathing hard from the struggle. He moved closer to the two strangers, sprawled on the ground.

Until then, he had never believed the people of the tower were real, had never thought he would live to see one of them. When he was younger, he believed the ghost stories. Later, he decided the sightings reported by some of his kin were in fact the Baron's people. But now there they were, two strange beings, two aliens in their strange gear, the faces inside the glass white and plump, clean shaven. So different.

As he stared, Sal's words echoed inside his skull. *Do not approach them. Hide.* But curiosity had the better of him. He stared. He studied them, the pained looks, the strange colour of their eyes. Behind him, his friends had calmed down and were now discussing what they should do. Tie them up, someone said, leave them there, the dogs and the rats would take care of the rest. Someone else suggested they should take them back to the temple and let

Sal decide. The latter argument won the favour of the majority.

They tied their hands and three of them stood guard while the others went down inside a house to bring out what Dalin and Pat had found earlier. After this task was done, they started walking back to the temple, the two prisoners now silent and subdued between them.

# 4 THE CELLAR

Sal went mad as soon as the Younglings walked in with the two captives.

Had they lost their minds, he asked. His hand slammed the table in front of him. He could not believe or even dare begin to understand how they could do exactly the opposite, *the opposite*, of what he had been preaching for years. How many times had he told them to steer clear of any strange people? How many times? And now they had captured them and brought them inside his home. Had the wind fried their brains? They had put a poisonous snake inside a bird's nest.

Edgar tried to jump in but there was no stopping the Taàr during an outburst of that kind. Sal told him to refrain from bringing up excuses. He told them to go, all of them, away, somewhere far from him. Then he changed his mind. Stay, he told them, he would leave instead. He didn't care what they did, but by the time he came back he wanted them to get rid of the captives. And with those last words he stormed out of the temple. All the witnesses to his outburst just stood there speechless. Everyone knew Sal was outspoken but they had rarely seen a similar tirade.

Kim walked over to Edgar, who stood there, looking miserable. Putting her arm round his shoulders, she told him very softly not to worry, that Sal would soon cool down. She gave him advice to take the prisoners to the cellar of the white house, right across the street from the temple. There they could lock them safely and stand guard. She assured him that once Sal returned, he would tell them what to do.

Uncle Sam, who had sat there through the entire rant, intervened before the boys could move. Pointing his finger at his own nephew, he ordered him to guard the prisoners by himself. He was going to have to stay locked up in the cellars with them alone.

For many, it would have been humiliating having to stay the night outside the temple. But the boy was not afraid, although his uncle's words did bite. In truth he had nothing to do with his friends' decision to take the two men back to the temple. He hadn't questioned their decision either, and because of this he felt a little responsible. *Maybe I should have spoken*, he thought. Resigning himself, he accepted the order without objection.

Head lowered, he followed Edgar, Dalin and the others outside, with the tower men bound and gagged between them. Following Kim's advice, they took them across the street to a house that looked like all the rest from the outside, with collapsed walls and roof. However, once inside, they accessed the cellars that lay underneath. These cellars, like those of other houses around the temple, could be locked up and were used by Sal's people to store food and items found in the zones.

It was still late afternoon. They walked the short way, climbed down the narrow stairway that led to the cellars, opened the padlock on the metal door with a key Dalin brought from the temple, and walked inside. The place stank of damp but the air was fresh and welcoming after the morning heat. Daylight, coming in from three small apertures near the ceiling, gave enough light to see by. A number of arches held a ceiling of stone slabs and separated the cellar in several areas stacked high with boxes and sacks full of cans and jars.

At the far end, opposite the door, three alcoves had been hewn in the live rock and were each enclosed by a metal gate. They put both prisoners inside an empty one, unbinding their hands before closing them in. Dalin secured the gate with the padlock he had removed earlier from the main door.

The prisoners uttered not a word. They seemed to be accepting all that was happening to them with an unnatural calmness, as if it was all expected. *What would I do in their place,* thought the boy. *I would scream and shout and fight with all my strength. Why don't they react?*

The Younglings sat down on the floor, their backs to a wall facing the three high apertures. They chatted quietly and kept the boy company until the light started to dim and fail. Then they got up and left. Just before it got dark, Dalin brought some food and a jar of water for him and the captives, then left with a solemn good night, hurrying back before the temple doors closed.

As soon as Dalin was gone, the boy locked the door from the inside, lit a candle, found some empty sacks and made a bed with them in a corner. He didn't want to eat yet, so he lay down to rest for a little while.

The candle had burned about an inch when he opened his eyes again. The little nap had done him good. He got up, opened one of the cans Dalin had brought, sat down on the sacks once more, and ate slowly and silently. He could not see the prisoners from where he lay since their side of the cellar was in complete darkness. However he could hear them breathe, and for a while he heard rustles and movement.

When he finished his food, he poured three glasses of water, drank one, then took the other two across the room. These are for you, he told the darkness. Two hands came out between the bars and took the proffered glasses, then a voice thanked him. The boy noticed the man standing behind the bars had removed his clothes. All he was wearing now were a short sleeved shirt and really short pants. He asked them if they wanted to eat, and the man said yes, they would be grateful for some food. The boy went back, opened the remaining cans, picked up the candle, and walked back to the cell. Again, the same man took both cans and handed one to his friend, who nodded thanks to the boy, then dipped his fingers in the can and started to eat.

The boy placed the candle on the floor in front of the iron gate, then started to move back towards his makeshift bed. But the man asked him to wait. He wanted to know his name.

Without turning, he answered his name was Ben.

The man spoke again. His name was Nel he said, and he was pleased to meet him. His friend, quietly eating at the back of the cell, was called Karl. Would he like to have a chat?

About what, Ben asked with suspicion. But he had turned around and walked back closer to Nel. He was both afraid they would try something to escape, and curious at the same time to know everything about these strange people.

Nel shrugged. Any subject, whatever Ben wanted to know. They would answer all his questions. Perhaps he had sensed the eagerness in the boy's eyes.

Ben sat down with crossed legs in front of them, and was quiet for a long time. What did they want, he asked finally. Why did they come out of the tower? What was *inside* the tower anyway? Had they really dropped the bomb?

Visibly taken aback by this last question, Nel shook his hands vigorously. No, of course not. Why did he ask this? Did he believe this to be the truth?

It was what Sal had told them, the boy replied.

The two men exchanged looks, then Nel turned back to Ben. They had stepped out of their tower in the hope they could meet with the boy and his people, to get to know them. They thought they could become friends, and perhaps convince those outside to go live with them inside the tower. There was enough space for everyone and life inside the building was much *much* better than outside.

His voice was soft, warm. Ben said nothing, so the man went on, describing the place in detail. In awe, he listened. Fresh food and water for everyone, every day. Large gardens with the last remaining trees, plants and flowers, at least to their knowledge. A place where children are loved, where they can play as children are supposed to, and learn to become better people.

But be warned, he told him, not all the people inside the tower agreed that people from outside should join them. There was a divide: two opposing groups. Himself, Karl and others were in favour because they felt it wasn't fair they could live in the safest place on the planet while Ben and his kin had to survive in a contaminated environment, struggling for food, dying of sickness that could easily be cured. They believed the Taàr's people should be given the same opportunities as those within the tower. They should be thought about their past, about what happened to their planet. In return, their presence in the tower would be of enormous value–not only would they give the tower people new hope, they would also provide answers to so many questions, of how evolution had made them capable of living in the intense radioactive environment where they thrived against all odds.

Ben did not understand what Nel intended about that last point, and told him as much. Nel explained that someone like him or Karl, or any person bred and raised in the tower wouldn't survive outside more than a year without adequate protection, let alone forty, fifty or sixty years.

Sal is seventy five, the boy told them. The two men exchanged glances in the flickering light of the candle. They were evidently surprised.

Nel did not resume talking. Instead he sat down, his face against the metal bars separating him from the boy. His eyes were strange, reflecting the dancing light from the candle. Silence stretched for a little while longer. Then, in his low voice, he asked Ben to trust him, to consider their offer, for the good of all. The Taàr's people would be rid of their misery, while the people inside the tower would make new friends and with their help, ensure their legacy.

Had he answered all his questions, asked Nel with a little smile. Or had he confused him more?

# 5 A GIFT FOR THE BARON

Loud knocking woke him up. Scrambling to his feet, he hurried to the door and unbolted it. Jim and Pat had come to replace him. Ben walked out in the early light of dawn and headed straight towards the temple to find Sal. He found him standing near the map, giving a few last orders to a group of ten men. The previous day's rage seemed to have gone from the old man's face. Ben waited patiently until Sal dismissed the group, then stepped forward. He told him he needed to speak to him.

The old man turned to face the map and

calmly started fixing small flags on it. After a little while he looked at the boy, but did not say anything. It was an invitation to speak.

Clearing his throat, Ben told him about the conversation with the two men. Their names were Nel and Karl, he said. But at that Sal's face grew dark with anger, almost like the day before. Ben noticed this, but hurried on before the old man could interrupt him. They were good people, with good intentions he explained, and they had sought them out to offer them help.

His voice hard and low, the Taàr asked the boy if he had been poisoned by those other fools in his group. What was this help they offered? He was curious now, what was it they promised?

Ben felt confident enough to go on. He answered that Nel and Karl told him they could offer them a better life inside the Nimbus Tower. They had fresh food and water, enough for everyone. No one would die of sickness.

The Taàr laughed bitterly. And the boy believed them? Everyone died of sickness in the end. Death is sickness. Life is sickness. All are infected.

But Ben could not accept this. Or perhaps he did not understand it. Maybe he did not believe a single word they said. Maybe it was all a lie. But he yearned for their words to be true, he hoped that all of them together could find a way to live a better life, a life similar to the one their ancestors had lived, the life before the events that Sal recalled so vividly.

The anger seemed to seep out of the old man's face. He grabbed his chair, turned it around, and sat astride it with his chest against the back of the chair. When he spoke, there wasn't any anger in his words, but a sweet sadness.

The episodes he liked to recall, the tales about a better time, were just that–tales, he told the boy. That age was gone forever. Nothing and no one could bring back the things swept away by the bombs.

There was only one truth in the world where they lived–to survive, they needed to face reality day after day. It was a sad truth, a gift from those that came before them, the same ones that lived in an earthly paradise but never appreciated anything they had. He insisted that they should never permit themselves to repeat the same mistake, never again. They could not afford to be lured into the same trap as their ancestors. A better life, comforts, luxuries, were exactly that–a trap, a catalyst for power, envy, hate. It is the nature of mankind, Sal preached, that a man always wants more than he has.

He stopped for breath. Than lowering his voice to a barely inaudible whisper, he said that only hardship and suffering could make them keep both legs firmly on the ground. Through suffering, a man keeps a check on reality and doesn't get lost in illusions. He knows what Ben is going through, he can understand him. But he would like Ben to understand *him*. Dreaming of a better life could only bring more pain.

What would they offer them, he asked again. Did they have something they really needed? Good food? Purified water? Was there a perfect world inside the tower, like the one that people like them created then annihilated?

No, he was wrong to think they could live a better life. Those were dangerous thoughts. Thoughts that imprisoned the mind and incarcerated the soul. The people of Tartarys, in their misery and suffering, were free. They lived day by day, suffering, struggling together, sharing the sadness that gripped them all–but *free*. And freedom was priceless.

Go back to work, he told him. Ben should continue from where he left the day before. Sal would decide the fate of the prisoners. Go back, and forget everything they said.

This last order was not delivered with the usual gruffness. Instead, for the first time, Sal had shown Ben a feeling he was not used to receive. Perhaps it was affection, the kind a father would perhaps show his son. But how should he know? He never knew his father, never experienced tenderness. And instead of feeling good about it, Sal's attitude had the opposite effect on him. He felt himself fill with a blind rage, anger towards that old man who wouldn't accept anyone's opinion but his own.

He turned on his heels without a word and walked out of the temple without even taking his water ration. He took the same road of the previous day and walked alone to the place where he had met Karl and Nel. He didn't need anybody. He wanted only to stay by himself.

Ben hurried on, stamping hard as if the land was to blame for everything. He located the mound he was working on, went up, and threw at it all the anger and resentment he had boiling inside, smashing and throwing things blindly, trying to get rid of that uncontrollable rage.

Those two people were offering them a

chance to a better life, a chance to stop losing lives of friends in absurd ways. And what did Sal do? The hard headed old fool went preaching about freedom, righteousness and how helpful and logical it was to suffer all your life.

But he couldn't accept that reasoning. Not now, not ever. If there was the slightest chance of improving their situation, then he wanted to give it a try, for him and for all his friends. He would do anything in his power to succeed.

Step by step, one concrete block after another, his thoughts fell in place like pieces of a giant puzzle, while his anger slowly simmered into solid determination.

Now he knew what needed to be done. And no one would dare stop him.

It was still early afternoon when he set off back to the temple. He knew that by the time he reached Tartarys he would find the place almost empty as the searching parties would still be out. Surely, Sal and Kim would be there–and his Uncle Sam as well. They rarely went more than a hundred steps away from the temple nowadays. With them he would also find the women and small children.

When he got near the road that led to the temple, the boy went off track and climbed his way from a different route until he came to the white building. He went down to the cellars but to his frustration, found the door locked from the outside. That meant only one thing. He was too late.

He went back up the stairs and crossed the road to the temple. He found Sal, standing by the door, in his pants, his bare chest revealing the heavy golden chain with the cross dangling from it and old scars that told tales of their own. He was calmly carving out a piece of dark wood with a pen knife. He stopped as soon as he spotted Ben, a look of puzzlement in his good eye.

The old man asked Ben why he had come back so early. It was back to the usual gruff old Sal, which suited the boy perfectly. It was what he was accustomed to. He replied with the words he knew the old man would be thrilled at hearing. He told Sal he was right. That was why he had to leave early, because his conscience wouldn't let him alone. Sal was right. He should never have given attention to those two, to their lies.

The hint of a satisfied smile appeared on Sal's lips as he returned his attention to the carving. Without changing the tone of his voice, he told the boy to take his water ration, the one he had missed that morning. It was his way of accepting Ben's apology.

But the boy wanted more from their conversation. He started to walk in, and as he brushed passed Sal, he stopped as if a thought had suddenly popped up in his mind. Putting worry and wonder in his tone, he asked Sal how they would deal with the prisoners now that they knew where to find them.

The old man did not stop carving this time. Calmly, he replied he had already taken care of everything. At around noon he had sent the rest of the Younglings to accompany the tower people to the Baron. Sal did not want to kill them, and that way the Baron would be in his debt.

Cold sweat trickled down Ben's spine, but outwardly he managed to keep his cool. Just hearing the Baron's name spoken had that effect on many. With a smile, he told Sal that they were as good as dead.

The Taàr didn't reply immediately. He seemed lost in thought. Then when he spoke he did so cautiously, choosing his words with care. He sent them to the Baron because he knew how much he needed them. Sal said the Baron was obsessed with the thought of getting inside that building–a childhood obsession he had never lost. And now Sal the Taàr had given the Baron a key to unlock his dream. Yes, probably both men would end up dead in the end, but that was for the good of all. Turning his solitary eye towards the boy he told him he should better get on with it and go drink that glass of water before he had second thoughts. And afterwards, he should go and help Pierre clean up the new stores given there was still ample time until sunset.

It was clear Sal did not want to talk any further, so Ben thanked him and went briefly inside to drink. The stores he had been asked to help clean were located behind the temple, in underground cellars identical to those of the white house. They were not new stores, not at all. But that is what they kept calling them as they were found and cleared much later than other ones. The people who had built the buildings surrounding the temple had built them all with underlying cellars. These were the perfect place to store food and drink and ensure these didn't spoil. In other cellars they stored wood and other stuff like candles and tools. The underground spaces had to be cleaned very often due to the dust that came in through the small windows they kept open day and night.

Once back outside the temple, Ben went

around the tall building, towards the new cellars. But as soon as he was hidden from view, he looked this way and that to ensure nobody was watching him, then broke into a run. He went downhill, took a couple of turns until he found an unused track from which he could leave the town unnoticed. When he thought it was safe, he tried to guess the direction Edgar's group had taken. From the little Sal had said he estimated the Younglings had left about an hour before he made it back from the zones. As a group they would be slow, so he assumed he would be able to move much faster and reach them in no time. He hoped he could do so before they got into the Baron's territory.

He knew Edgar and Dalin. They were lazy, and a task such as that one meant they would do their best to make it as long as possible. He hoped his guesses were right.

As he ran on through the desolated streets, with the molten tarmac reformed in strange ugly black waves, the hot wind blowing incessantly against his face, he removed all thoughts from his mind. Instead, he concentrated on his heartbeat, quick and loud in his chest. After a little while the heat went to his head.

The boy didn't know what would happen once he found his friends. And he didn't want to think about it. He would need to improvise, depending on what he found. What he knew for sure was that he had no intention of hurting anyone, but he was determined to free the two captives at the cost of having to do something undesirable. He wanted to seek the truth in the words Nel spoke when they were in the cellar.

Through the morning's exchange with the old Taàr, Ben had found renewed motivation, a determination that grew and solidified and became a reason for living.

He ran and ran for what seemed like forever without catching a glimpse of anyone. He was so parched he felt pain when he tried to swallow his own spit. The sweat oozing out of every pore had drenched his clothes completely.

He persisted even though the thought he had taken a wrong route grew stronger with every minute. He was still in the Taàr's territory, although he had rarely ventured this far before. Abolishing the thought of satisfying his thirst from his mind, Ben trudged on. And finally, he found them.

The first thing he spotted was a movement in the near distance, which made him take a sharp turn into a secondary path. Using this way, he ran on parallel to the main road until he had covered some distance. Then he stopped and hid to wait for them and confirm they were who he wanted them to be. To his great relief, the Younglings came into view.

Dalin and Pat were at the front, then came the captives, dressed once more in their strange gear, hands tied in front of them. Edgar and Alex brought up the rear, chatting in whispers. And now came the difficult part. How was he going to distract his friends long enough to set free the two men?

He opened the pocket where he kept the empty bags, the torch light and a flare gun that every one of them carried for emergencies. All of the items they possessed were a relic of a distant past that like many other things they found buried in the underground cities, once the pinnacle of civilization. Ben took out the gun and tried to calculate the risks if he had to fire a shot in their midst. Perhaps they would disperse, but they could take the two men with them. They would also understand immediately that it was one of their own shooting at them as the Baron's clan didn't use flare guns. And finally, there was the possibility that he could injure them. So he changed his mind and pocketed the gun.

*Think quick*, he told himself as he watched them go by. Then an idea sprang from nowhere and he thought it could work. He rummaged in the same pocket until he found a piece of cloth, one of those they used as flags to mark a spot. He crawled back until he was hidden completely and broke into a run to get ahead of them once more.

He came upon an open space which his friends would inevitably have to cross and found a good hiding spot at the far end. He took off the mask and stuffed it in the pocket with the other things. Instead of the mask, he tied the red cloth so it fitted tightly over his nose and mouth. He didn't have long to wait. The group of six people came into view, walking through the middle of the clearing. No one was talking now. Actually, they looked nervous, perhaps because that clearing marked a sort of boundary between the Taàr's and the Baron's territories.

The land was divided in two roughly equal territories, with the Nimbus tower marking the centre. The north belonged to the Taàr, the south to the Baron's clan. And that was the reason Edgar had picked that road, as it was the shortest and surest route.

Ben didn't know much about the people living in those areas or about their leader, other than hearsay. It was said that Burak, known to everyone as the Baron, was a giant, strong and fierce. His people ate rats, and dogs, and sometimes humans. Even their own dead. That was what Sal and the older ones said. Ben didn't care to find out.

Rorik had met Burak the Baron only once. He had described him as being younger than Sal, perhaps ten years his junior, and he used to say his look scared the shit out of him. That one time, the Baron was accompanied by a dozen armed guards. The boy had heard from many sources that once Sal and Burak were close friends, until something happened that got them separated.

When the Younglings reached the centre of the open space, Ben placed his hands on the cloth covering his mouth. Without getting up, he started shouting in a loud voice to stop where they were. Thanks to the cloth, his voice came out distorted–muffled and strong, much different from his normal voice.

The six people in the plaza froze in their tracks. Ben continued to shout. He asked them to state their business, to give a valid reason for their presence on the Baron's land. He stopped speaking and his voice echoed for a while, then a dead silence followed.

After a long moment Dalin's reply filled the silence. He could not see the boy, but Ben could see him very clearly, looking this way and that, trying to spot the speaker.

They had been sent by Sal the Taàr, Dalin shouted back. They brought two men from the white tower with them, as captives. A gift to the Baron from his friend the Taàr.

Ben did not reply immediately. He let a few quiet moments go by until he saw his friends fidgeting nervously, moving from one foot to the other. When he thought he had waited long enough, he told Dalin to leave the captives there, in the middle of the plaza, and go back. After a moment's hesitation, he saw

Edgar order Pat, Dalin and Alex do as bidden.

Nel and Karl were left there, standing alone, hands tied, looking around them, seeming lost. Again Ben waited. Then he ordered the two men to advance towards a side street to their right. They obliged.

He had done this to avoid being seen by his friends should they have stayed hidden somewhere close by to watch. Slowly, the two men advanced, until they were directly below him. He ran down the mound, took out a pen knife, and cut the rope. Then he removed the cloth covering half his face. If they were surprised at seeing him, they didn't show it.

He asked them to hurry, to follow him quickly as time was against them, then started moving south east, deeper into Baron's territory. He looked back, and noticed Nel and Karl were not following him. They just stood there, baffled. Come on, he urged them again. Follow me.

They moved, reaching him with a few quick strides. Nel put a hand on Ben's shoulder and thanked him for what he had done. But it was enough. He should go now, leave them to their own devices. Otherwise he would be missed by his own people, and when he got back he would have a lot of explaining to do.

I'm not going back, Ben replied. And they should better hurry up unless they wanted to be found by the Baron's people for real. They were not as sweet with their captives as the Taàr's people. They might even end up in a cook pot.

But Nel seemed not to comprehend. Or perhaps he did not want to. He looked back at Ben and asked him where he intended to go if not back to his clan. Where would he live?

With them, in the tower, Ben replied, and it was not a request.

Nel and Karl looked at each other and seemed to speak without words. Then Nel turned back to the boy and moved his head in an affirmative way. Very well, he said. Let's go.

# 6 OVER THE THRESHOLD

The colossal structure could be seen from every corner of the island, by day and also by night. Apart from the immensity of its proportions, the pure white walls shone bright during the day, reflecting the sun's rays that somehow managed to penetrate the thick clouds. At night, the whole building glowed with a soft bluish light. Because of this, it was easy for them to pick the right direction.

No one spoke as they walked. They kept to secondary roads as much as possible, their ears open for any sound of trouble. Night came upon them quickly, obscuring their vision completely, until all they could see was the bluish column to their north east. The wind blew unrelenting, unceasing.

Ben felt hungry and terribly thirsty. His throat was so parched that he knew he wouldn't be able to speak if he tried. He couldn't help but think that on any other day, by that time, he would have already eaten the daily meal and probably lay down to sleep or to listen to one of Sal's stories. That thinking didn't help, so instead he tried to focus on their current situation.

They were now moving so slowly that they seemed like three toddlers just learning to walk. Or like the three blind mice, Nel said. Did Ben know that story? Ben replied he did not and for a little while, Nel's voice drifted across the pitch black in a low murmur, reciting the ancient rhyme. Then it was back to silent walking. It wasn't possible to move faster–the darkness was solid around them. The boy held the torch light in his hand and every now and then switched it on for a few seconds to point the way. He wouldn't dare leaving it on for longer, as it would draw unwanted attention.

Then all of a sudden, the growling and barking started. Afraid, Ben switched on the light and wished he hadn't. Tens of pairs of ferocious eyes caught the light and shimmered at them from every side. And underneath each green pair of eyes, there was a jaw full of sharp teeth, frothing with anticipation. There was no way to run.

The barking was so loud, the growling a roar. The dogs attacked as one without giving their prey a chance to think or do anything. The boy switched off the light but knew it would not help. So in the same split second switched it back on and found a massive canine head with a wide open jaw ready to snap his face . . .

. . . and the dog just stopped. All the attacking beasts stopped simultaneously, crying as if whipped and beaten. With their tails between their legs they withdrew back into the night until there was no sign of them.

Bewildered and shocked, Ben just stood there, shaking. He could not believe he had just escaped certain death. He pointed the light around him in a complete circle until it fell on Nel and Karl. Nel asked him to switch it off, and he did so immediately. He was right, the light gave their position away.

What had just happened, he asked the darkness.

And the darkness answered back in an unfamiliar voice that they had used a special whistle they kept hidden in a secret pocket in their jackets. This was the first time he had heard Karl speak–his voice was hoarse, rasping. He waited for more details but none came. Apparently, Karl was a man of few words. Ben accepted the answer, although he was curious to know more about this special whistle. Such a tool would be priceless for his clan. If they had one, tens, maybe hundreds of lives would have been spared. But since Karl wasn't going to provide more information, he didn't ask for more. He wasn't in the mood for talking either.

Nel encouraged them to proceed, and soon they were on their way again towards the pale blue column in the distance. Time dragged by, and their progress seemed stalled. Their going was too slow. In constant fear of more surprises, they persevered warily, losing their way, retracing their steps, going on. Tiredness set in, but they couldn't stop. So step after step they marched silently onwards.

Finally the first hint of dawn tinged the clouds to the east. Gradually, visibility improved and they started moving faster.

Slowly, the tower grew larger. Every time his gaze fell upon it, Ben felt bewildered by what he saw. Although he had been constantly aware of the presence of the tower ever since he was big enough to understand, he had always seen it from far off. He knew it was big. Some said enormous. But he had never really grasped the meaning of enormous. Now he understood.

When he commented on this, the two men smiled. They had never imagined that the people living outside would find their tower so enigmatic and symbolic.

They stopped talking without agreeing to. And in that silence Ben took in his surroundings inch by inch. The territory was unfamiliar, although the scenery familiar. The streets looked like those he grew up in, the rubble heaps identical. Perhaps, he thought, the closer they got to the tower the more severe the damage had been, but maybe it was his imagination. He did not ask. It was not important.

Now that the tower filled his entire view, he couldn't help but notice that the steep curved walls of the white tower were perfectly smooth. Those walls rose out of the rocky ground and climbed vertically up and up, disappearing into the reddish clouds. He imagined them made of some white glass that reflected the light until his eyes hurt, even though there were no direct sun rays.

The sun. In his tales, Sal described the sun as a ball of fire that moved up from the eastern horizon burning red, then it yellowed as it crossed all the sky and went down at the opposite side. He had seen pictures, and knew exactly how to imagine it, although he yearned to see it with his own eyes someday. *Perhaps*, he thought, *from the top of the tower one could look above the clouds . . .*

The rubble and destruction stopped suddenly about a mile away from the base of the tower. That base was so wide, that he estimated it would take him from sunup to sundown to go around it.

They came out into an immense empty expanse that the boy noticed immediately had been cleared of everything. The vast emptiness added to the solitude of the place. To their left, dwarfed by the white walls, lay what appeared to be a walled round area. A cemetery, Nel told him, for burying the dead.

The concept was alien to the boy, but he

refrained from commenting. This close to the tower his mind was occupied with absorbing the immensity of the building itself.

He felt so small, so insignificant. How had such a construction been built? How long had it taken? How many people had worked on it?

Nel and Karl led him on towards some kind of doorway that looked tiny from a distance. Close up it was wider than the temple he grew up in. Without knocking or doing anything, a much smaller door opened noiselessly within the larger frame. They passed inside.

Ben's last thought as he stepped over the threshold was whether Sal was right in his judgement of the people inside the tower. Now he was going to find out by himself.

# Part Two

# The Nimbus Tower

# 7 ANOTHER LIFE

A sound so beautiful, so soft. He thought he was hearing the voices of angels speaking. Never had he heard anything of the sort. Such wonder. His heart filled with a joy he had never known.

Music. That's what they told him it was. He had never heard music. Sal told them about it, and always said that it was a nice thing to hear, but Ben could never have imagined it so beautiful . . .

. . . then sleep embraced him completely.

He came slowly to his senses, gradually gaining consciousness in a white-walled room that was bright, clean, silent and fresh.

The music played on, but Ben knew that what he was hearing was only a remnant of the tune he heard the day he entered the tower. And that thought made him wonder.

How long had he been in there? Ben could not remember. He felt it had been only a very short time, but couldn't be certain why he felt that way. His mind was kind of fuzzy which made it difficult to form any thoughts. It was like that one time when Sal let them taste a drink they had found during one of their scavenging trips. A dark liquid, sweet and full of flavour. It had muddled his thoughts shortly after drinking a small glass. Sal had warned him he would feel strange for a while, and laughed at him when he started babbling.

Ben closed his eyes. In the darkness he could think better. A strange smell drifted up to him. A strange *nice* smell. Opening his eyes again he tried to take in his surroundings. A white sheet covered him up to his neck. It rustled softly as he moved. A pillow of the same white cloth as the bed sheets propped up his head. He smelt the linen. It smelled good but it was not the same smell that had engulfed his senses when he closed his eyes. He peeked under the bed sheet and found he was wearing only short clean underpants. The nice smell was wafting off his own skin. He realised someone had washed him.

And suddenly he remembered. They had asked him to take off all of his clothes, then he went into a glass chamber and was doused with large amounts of soapy warm water. The shower had felt so good, and it lasted for a very long time. *What a waste*, he remembered thinking. He had never washed himself like that. Water was too scarce a resource to waste that way. And more often than not it would be contaminated, making you itch and scratch.

After that shower that took off fourteen years of dirt and grime, Nel led him to a well lit room. On one side, two huge windows faced inwards, towards the hollowed out centre of the tower. A beautiful light camc in from these windows and he walked up to them to have a look. He remembered feeling sick when he saw the great depth underneath him. Storey upon storey upon storey, each one with its own triangular terrace that jutted out in a sort of immense spiral staircase so that each one had its own share of light from above.

Those terraces. He had been so amazed at the sight of the lush green plants and trees that grew upon those triangular pieces of heaven. In some of them, he noticed movement and realised that people the size of ants were down there, walking around. He had never thought he would ever see real vegetation in his lifetime. Some of the trees down there must have been gigantic, especially those on the lower terraces. Are those forests, he had asked Nel. But the man had laughed. No, but they are the best next thing, he had replied.

When Ben had raised his eyes upwards he had seen rays of sunlight coming through a huge opaque glass dome. Nel left him alone as he took in all this, returning a while later with a tray that held food and a yellowish drink in a large glass.

He still remembered the explosion of taste as he gave the first bite, and devoured it without ever asking what it was. The drink was sweet, that was all he remembered about it.

Closing his eyes once more, he took deep long breaths. The air felt so clean, so good. And now that he was once again in darkness, he heard sounds he knew he had also heard that first day in the tower. Chirping and calling–the sounds made by birds. He had watched them transfixed as they flew free from tree to tree, from terrace to terrace, flying, gliding, diving through the air.

Had it all been a dream?

Taking out his legs from beneath the

sheets he swung them to the floor and pushed himself up. His head spinned and his muscles ached. Maybe he wasn't used to sleeping on something that comfortable he thought, or maybe it was a sign of how long he had been asleep in the same position.

The room was quite large, with two beds facing each other. Next to each bed there was a small shelf affixed to the wall. There was nothing else. Everything was white–the beds, the sheets, the door, the window frame. The door was to his right. It did not have any hinges or knobs and he remembered that doors in the tower opened magically when you approached them, sliding inside the wall.

But what really caught his attention was once again the open window set in the wall to his left. It was nearly as wide as the whole room, and through it came the soft glare from the sun above and the sweet unfamiliar noises made by birds and other creatures. He went over to gaze once again upon that vision from a dream he never dared to dream, at the lush greenery and swooping birds. Ben breathed in the damp pure air, so conscious of the absence of that forsaken wind and clouds of dust that had been a part of his life as much as the clothes he used to wear.

He heard a soft sound from behind him, as if two things rubbed against each other, and turned to look. He saw the door sliding to the left, inside the wall, exactly as he remembered. It revealed a tiny figure: a boy, all smiles upon a face as white as the bed sheets that lay crumpled on his bed. He judged him to be a few years younger than himself, ten, maybe twelve inches shorter, but stocky. His hair seemed made of gold, a colour he had never seen before on other people.

"Good morning!" the boy said with a beaming smile as he walked straight in and went to sit on the other bed. "You must be Ben. I'm Russ. This is my bed you know, cause from today we're sharing the same room. Isn't it amazing?"

He was wearing clothes similar to what Nel and Karl had worn once they were back in the tower, with the addition of a wide belt of brown material around his waist. He was barefoot. For a moment, Russ stopped talking and looked at Ben as if expecting him to say something, but after a few seconds he took a deep breath and started chattering again.

"Would you like me to take you around the tower when you're feeling better? It's huge you know! I've never managed to visit it all even though I'm ten. I can take you to see the school and the library, the games room, the chapels, the swimming pools–we can swim in them if you want. Can you swim? The roof is a must. You have to see the view from up there. It's really breath taking. Will you tell me stories about what's out there, maybe about what it's like to live in the desolation? I can show you lots of movies that show how the world was before the attacks. I'm sure you'd like that."

He stopped, as if suddenly realising

something for the first time. Russ inclined his head slightly to the right, like a curious rat.

"You do speak don't you?" he asked. "Do you understand me?"

Ben turned to face the window, and without looking at Russ, pointed towards the terraces and asked him if he could take him there.

Russ got up from the bed and went to look at what Ben was pointing at. He had to get up on his toes to look out the window.

"You want to go near the trees?"

Ben replied by moving his head.

"Come, let's go now. But first you must wear something you know. We're not allowed to go around like that in the tower."

And what should he wear, Ben asked. He didn't have any clothes.

Russ walked up to Ben's bed and facing the shelf fixed to the wall he pressed his hand slightly above it. A large part of wall on the same side of the bed opened up to reveal a walk-in wardrobe. Hanging inside were two identical sets of clothes, exactly like the one Russ was wearing.

Taking the first one, he tried it on. It fitted him almost perfectly. He did not ask for shoes given that Russ wasn't wearing any. He wasn't used to walk around barefoot, but was willing to give it a try.

"Come on, let's go!" Russ urged him, jumping from one foot to the other, barely containing his enthusiasm.

In the evening of that same day, Ben found himself once more lying face up on his bed in his room within the tower. On the bed opposite his, Russ lay snoring and sometimes chattering incomprehensibly in his dreams. Ben however could not sleep.

He thought that perhaps the excitement was keeping him awake. On that first day as an official resident of the tower he had seen, heard, smelled and touched things he never believed he would in his lifetime. Some of those things he knew about from Sal's tales or from pictures he had seen. But other things were completely new to him, and some needed time to comprehend. He closed his eyes once more and tried to remember the strong yet pleasant smell of the yellow fruit Russ had called a lemon, the sour taste of another similar fruit but bigger, more rounded and almost reddish in colour. He remembered the sweet taste of the small red fruit that he forgot the name of. He had felt reborn among those trees and plants, each one with its own particular smell and shape. And then, upon the branches within the trees, he saw those magnificent creatures that he envied for being able to fly so gracefully and effortlessly. Their colours hypnotized him, their different calls made his ears burst with pleasure.

When an older man saw the boy's fascination with the birds, he started teaching him about the various species and particular characteristics of each one. He told him that the birds he was seeing were just a fraction of what once existed in the whole world.

In some of the terraces Russ showed him other animals and insects, like rabbits, tame dogs that at first he wouldn't dare touch, cats, turtles and tortoises, large docile funny looking animals with a soft white woollen coat that he fed from his own hands. In another terrace he spent hours staring at the clear water of a giant lake size pool full of fish and water plants called lilies, with white butterflies flying from one flower to another and even small green creatures that jumped away when he went near them.

The tower *was* a very large building, by far bigger than he could ever have imagined when he had looked at it from afar in his previous life. He discovered that the tower had been designed by an older generation to withstand disasters, natural or man-made. A prototype they had called it, although he did not know what it meant.

The outer layer, the material that gave the tower its brilliant white look, was indeed a type of glass. It was specially made to collect energy from the sun to generate electricity for consumption by the inhabitants of the tower. The white glass was extremely resistant to high temperatures and to impacts, as well as being able to stop harmful radiation from entering the tower.

Within the top floors, in specially built rooms called glass houses, the tower people cultivated fruit and vegetables for consumption. Water for irrigation was collected from rain and dew and from recycled water filtered through complex processes in the basement of the tower from where it was pumped back up. And when he asked about the seeds he was told that they saved a portion from every crop to retain seeds, but they also had a reserve that was worth more than gold or diamonds to them.

Gold and diamonds meant nothing to Ben. Water and food did. But this time he understood what the little Russ meant. Sal had told them how their ancestors were concerned about money and riches.

The rain and dew were collected at the base of the tower. Water would slide down the outer walls and seep through special collection systems underground.

Collected water was then circulated through several different levels of filtering as it went down towards the large reservoirs built deep underneath the tower, where it was treated further and kept clean. Then, the same as recycled water, it would be pumped up again to be consumed.

Russ took him up to the roof late in the afternoon. He took him outside, even if for just a minute, as Russ could not stay long outside the tower without his protective gear. The people of the tower knew the dire effects radiation would have on them. Anyway, the strong winds wouldn't have let them stay longer than that since they could hardly even breathe–even those winds, he had been told, were a side affect of the atomic bombing. But for just a minute, Ben saw two images he would remember for the rest of his life. The setting sun was one. A deep orange ball, hazy in the west, sliding rapidly behind a sea of dark purple clouds. The other was the clouds themselves, seen from above rather than below.

Back inside, Russ still had one more place to take him–a long and narrow room several floors down, just beneath the blanket of clouds. This served as a belvedere with the wall facing outwards made of clear see-through glass. Within the inwards stone wall, alcoves were set every ten paces where people could sit and admire the view. If there still had been a view.

For the first time in his life, he found himself looking at the land that gave him birth. From those heights, he was able to see nearly the whole island from end to end, and even a glimpse of the dead water beyond. It was both horrifying and amazing at the same time. Amazing because it wasn't a view he saw every day, horrifying because it displayed the full extent of the damage done by the explosion. He understood now why the people of the tower called the zones the Desolation. It made sense.

The landscape looked so bleak. It alternated between patches of black, dark grey and a lighter grey, the colour of ash. No trees, not even weed grew. The demolished buildings that for years he had worked so hard to get into looked ghostly from that height. A darkness fell over his heart as he took it all in. He knew that once, in a past that seemed very distant now, what lay before him had been a perfect world, a paradise shared by every inhabitant. He knew this truth now existed only in Sal's stories.

He asked Russ to take him away from there. He couldn't take it any longer. The experience tainted a little the enjoyment of the rest of the afternoon, but it did not take it away completely. On that first day he had only seen a very small part of the tower, but on the following days, Russ took him to every corner he had access to. He showed him things that blew his mind, told him all he knew about the history of his people and of the tower in which he was born, introduced him to so many people that he had trouble remembering their faces, let alone their names.

Together they spent whole afternoons in the pools, where Russ patiently tried to teach him to swim. He had not yet grasped the concept but just splashing around in the water was enough for him. Many a night Russ took him to a special room with deep soft seats. There they sat with other people and watched stories on a screen. Russ called these movies, explaining that their ancestors used to create them for entertainment.

One morning, Russ woke him up very early, saying he had a surprise for him. Outside was still dark. The kid, full of excitement, chattered away so fast that Ben could hardly understand him. He heard the word 'glider' repeatedly, together with 'races' and a lot of 'come on let's go' while tugging his hand to make him follow.

Putting on his clothes as quickly as he could, he followed Russ out of their room, through empty corridors and silent lifts, up and up until they reached the top most floor. They went inside a massive hall, one they had visited once before. On that occasion, it had been empty. Now it was crowded with people and some sort of equipment that lay sprawled over several areas on the polished floor. There was a vibe in the air, he could feel it, like a beating pulse, full of life.

Russ moved in with the crowd, excited, unstoppable. It took Ben a long time to finally understand that on that day there was going to be a glider race. It was an event held three or four times a year in which everyone could participate. The gliders were like wide triangular wings of canvas set on a very light frame that was strong enough to carry two persons side by side. For the race, each glider would have only one rider. They would drop off into the central empty space of the tower, and the rider who remained longest in the air would be declared winner. Every glider had its own unique design and colour, and when one by one they set off into the air, spiralling down like huge birds over a current of air, the watcher's eyes were presented with a marvellous view of dancing colours.

Ben enjoyed himself so much that he soon joined the crowd, shouting encouragement to the participants, clapping hands to an improvised chorus, cheering and laughing. On that morning there were eleven competitors, some of them quite old, others maybe twice the age of the boy. However they all shared the same innocent pleasure, laughing with joy as they went down in circles. A middle aged man called Martin with white at his temples won the game. He was the last in the air, and even though he knew to be the winner he kept gliding on and on and all the time the crowd cheered and applauded and shouted praise at him from above.

It was a festive occasion for all the people

of the tower, one in which Ben saw the people in a different light. He saw the unity between them, the joy they shared, the feelings they expressed towards each other. The winner was praised and cheered in that same hall and for a long time they stayed there, joking, talking, having fun together. He was amazed at how adults enjoyed themselves and behaved like children.

During these celebrations, gliders were available for who ever wanted to ride them. Ben discovered that Russ had been learning to fly one for the past two years, and without knowing exactly how, he found himself strapped in beside his little friend.

"Now just hold tight with your hands and relax the rest of your body. I'll take care of the rest."

He wasn't going to argue and did as he was bid. They jumped off the edge of the top most parapet and with skill, the kid flew the glider in slow wide spirals down and down. It was the most fabulous experience of his life.

It was amazing gliding past the top of the tallest trees, watching them come nearer and nearer, then brushing past within inches of them. Birds flew around them and he felt as if his wish to one day fly free like those creatures had come true much earlier than expected.

Days and nights went by.

Nel appeared early one morning when Ben was still asleep in bed, in the room he now called his own. Russ was not there–his bed was unmade, as if he had woken up in a hurry.

He had not seen the man since the day after he came in the tower. Ben was glad to see him and told him so. Nel bid him good morning in his usual smile.

Ben wanted to know where Nel had been for all that time. He had asked for him but no one seemed to have an answer. He wanted to tell him he had been right. Life in the tower was so much better than how he had lived in the Desolation.

It was so easy for him to become accustomed to that way of life. There were some things he still felt were extravagant, he told Nel, but apart from that, the only thing that bothered him was missing his friends, especially late at night before going to bed.

Nel went around the bed and sat down beside him. He was glad that the boy was enjoying the tower. He had been sure he would feel at home in no time, although he could imagine how certain customs were not easy to assimilate. But they could talk those things over, and they could also speak of his friends. Now he wanted him to get up and go spend the day with him, starting with breakfast. What did Ben think of that idea, Nel wanted to know. Would he join him?

Ben jumped out of bed and put on the clothes he had thrown over the bedside shelf the night before. They walked together to the dining hall, a place where some time or other one would meet every inhabitant of the tower.

For breakfast they had a bun of dark grain each and as much water as they desired. For one who had never tasted bread in his life, that meagre meal was a godsend, one he looked forward to every morning with great anticipation.

Nel ate his bun in two bites and continued talking.

Now that some time had passed, it was clear from Ben's words that he had had enough time to compare this life with his previous one outside those walls. He was sure Ben could see that within the confines of the tower there was meaning to their existence, that it was not just a question of survival like life in the Desolation. But before going on, he wanted to ask him a question. Had he noticed something out of the ordinary during the time he had been in the tower? Something unnatural perhaps?

Ben laughed so hard that he started to cough and it took him a long time to calm down enough to be able to speak. Was Nel serious? Did he really think he could mention just one thing that was out of the ordinary? A comfortable bed was strange, or the dark bread he ate every morning. The trees and the animals, the artificial lights at night, or simply the fact that he could have a shower before going to bed. Everything was alien to him. The question should have been put otherwise–was there anything normal? And then he could have answered that no, nothing was normal inside the tower. He started laughing again, jumping up and down on his chair.

Nel joined him, laughing and enjoying seeing the boy so happy. He commented on how much Ben had changed in the short time he had been in the tower, how full of life he had become.

Ben was right. His question was not about the things the boy mentioned. What he had in mind was something much more specific. He wanted to know whether Ben noticed something peculiar amongst the people of the tower. Did Russ mention anything?

Ben stopped laughing and concentrated while he took another bite of bread, munching it thoughtfully.

Finally he asked Nel if he was referring to the fact that there were no children younger than Russ. Now that he thought about it, the greater part of the men in the tower were old, and he had never seen any women.

No, he had not seen, nor would he see, any women in the tower. Russ was indeed the youngest. Would he care to know the whole story? To an enthusiastic nod of the boy's head, Nel began his revealing tale of the odd history of the Nimbus tower–one that Russ had never mentioned.

Although Nel was fifty five years old, he was not yet born when the story he would now be telling began. However, he knew every detail, chiefly thanks to the chronicles written by the previous generation–his parents among them.

The written testimony of what those

people saw with their own eyes over seventy years in the past was a vivid and moving story that still evoked feelings of desperation and great sadness every time Nel read it. The tale begins on the day the first atomic bomb was launched, on the 7th of August.

In an ancient building, that was now just another heap of rubble in the Desolation, the five great leaders of that era met for what was meant to be a historical event. On their agenda lay a number of important decisions regarding the ever increasing conflicts between north Africa and Europe. An enemy still unknown to that day took the opportunity to get rid of all five leaders in a coordinated attack. No one knows the real intention of the attackers, but some think that the bombardments went out of proportion. Others believe that the real intention was always to wipe away humanity once and for all, and the meeting of the five leaders was only a pretext, or possibly, just a coincidence. No one knows exactly. What is certain is that the attackers must have had access to a vast atomic arsenal.

The attack on their country was only the first of many other known bombings that took place all over the world on the same day. It was genocide, on a global scale.

Nel said the chronicles described that first bomb, the one that devastated the island, as it fell from the sky and exploded one kilometre above ground, six or seven kilometres away from the tower. The end result could still be seen by everyone. On the island alone, more than two million people died instantly, most of them burned to cinders where they stood by the heat of the blast, others buried alive in their homes, public places or while working.

A hundred thousand souls lived the day. Many of them knocked on the doors of the tower. But those doors never opened. Even if the people inside the building wanted to help, they could not do so. The doors were automatically sealed and would not open for at least six months–it was a pre-cautionary measure made by design and there was no way to manually override it.

Ben asked what this meant, and Nel obliged immediately. The building they were in, he explained, was unique. It was built as a collaborative experiment by a group of scientists from around the world to create the first fully autonomous self-sufficient tower city in the world. A building that could withstand natural or manmade disasters, to sustain and preserve life without needing anything from the outside. Similar attempts were made with bio spheres in the twenty first century, but they were unsuccessful, mainly due to the high running costs. The tower project, codenamed Project Nimbus, attempted to overcome these financial issues. Governments from around the world participated in the project, and the resources were easily found. If successful, Project Nimbus would be the master plan for other such towers around the globe. And it was successful. Beyond any expectation.

The doors were automatically sealed off by a mechanism set in motion the instant the nuclear weapon was activated. Nel quoted from a report written by Professor Jordan. In his report, the professor stated that the tower rocked to and fro with the force of the blast for several hours that day. But the building held intact while everything around it was devastated.

The survivors within the tower numbered almost three thousand–at that point the building was nearing completion, but still works-in-progress. Once it was finished, it would have offered residence to a hundred thousand souls.

Out of those three thousand there were several scientists but also builders and workers who were working within the structure at the time. Their families and friends died a horrible death while they were untouched inside the experiment they had been building for future generations. They soon realised they had become part of that same experiment.

After the six months passed, no one went out. The survivors had long since stopped coming knocking on the tower doors and everyone assumed they were all dead. The effects of an atomic weapon were well known. Radioactive poisoning was so high that no creature could possibly live with the exception of some insects known for their resilience to radiation.

So they lived on, in confinement, eating the vegetables they cultivated themselves, drinking purified water, and studying the effects of that disaster. After all, went on Nel, a scientist is always a scientist, and will observe anything given the opportunity.

Aware that he had talked too much, Nel stopped at that point. He suggested they should go and continue their conversation somewhere else, and Ben, fascinated and intrigued by Nel's story, agreed without hesitation.

# 8 NEL'S REQUEST

He had never been to the place Nel took him next. Some areas within the tower were restricted to Russ, and this was one of them. Nel had to open three doors to get through, each one unlocking with an eye reading mechanism Nel called an eye scanner. Behind the third door they found a hall so vast that objects and people on the other side looked tiny.

Large windows on the inner wall looked over one of the terraces while far on the opposite side, Ben thought the walls looked slightly curved. He thought that perhaps that was the outer wall of the tower. However, there were no visible windows over that side.

Total silence reigned supreme, even though there were other people in the hall besides themselves. Columns supported the immense roof, while a solitary round room with transparent glass walls sat at the very centre. Rows of benches in a star shaped formation jutted out from that centre in all directions. The benches nearest to Ben contained strange looking devices and equipment full of little green, red, blue and yellow lights. Half a dozen men were seated in front of those devices, looking silently at them. Far away, beyond the last benches, people moved to and fro among a shelved section. He couldn't tell what the shelves contained from that distance.

That hall was the heart of the scientist's experiment, Nel explained, the place that controlled all the functions of the building, an observatory of tiny little details that worked together to ensure that the vertical city could remain whole. From within that place, day after day, the scientists who survived the atomic attack measured and studied the effects of the nuclear disaster. They grew old and died but their work was carried on by the next generations of scientists, who strived to keep a watchful eye upon the outside world.

Nel stopped and turned to the boy.

And after they grew old and died, he said, there would be no one left to continue the legacy.

The man could not keep the sadness out of his voice as he said those last words. It was so strong Ben felt a sudden urge to cry. Those words were important to the man in front of him. In that instant he understood that Nel's story, the one he had not yet finished telling, had arrived at a critical point, and he dreaded what was coming next.

But the sadness lifted suddenly from Nel, as if he had had a change of heart, and instead he changed subject completely. He asked Ben to follow him and they made their way across the hall to the shelved section. As they walked, Nel started explaining that those shelves held years of research and reports, containing within them meticulous observations and calculations.

The scientists recorded every tiny detail, he said. Their job was to compare gathered data, analyse changes and predict outcomes.

It was difficult for Ben to understand but he listened intently and watched everything.

The man and the boy continued their tour around the hall. They reached the round glass room at the centre, which Nel said was a laboratory for dangerous or potentially harmful experiments.

They walked on. They went through a section where miniature cities were displayed on waist-high stands. Nel explained that the models showed areas of the island before and after the bombardments and were done by a device called a model printer, which Nel would be showing him later.

Would he like to see the place where he had grown up? Ben said yes, and Nel showed him a model of an intact  town, the familiar temple towering above beautiful little houses all painted in different colours, with tiny doors and windows, the streets clear and neat. The boy stared at the model for a long time. Then he nodded, and they went on.

An old man looked up from the biggest book Ben had ever seen, nodded silently to them, and carried on reading. They reached wide double glass doors and passed through them onto the lowest terrace. The doors closed behind them.

A current of humid warm air greeted them, together with a thousand morning calls of different birds shuffling through the branches of the tall trees. Compared to the artificial air inside the hall, this was quite different. From high above, sunlight drifted faint and opaque, giving a pastel-like nature to the lush green environment.

Although Ben had gone on the terraces

many times, he felt renewed amazement every single time he saw the towering trees, the creatures flying, the grass and the flowers. He would feel an inexpressible happiness take hold of him.

This particular terrace was the largest of all, with so many trees packed together and tight winding passages between them. They picked a passage and walked in silence for some time, until Nel pointed to the tallest tree the boy had ever seen. An oak, according to Nel. He suggested they stop there and as soon as they were seated, Nel resumed his story.

Where was he? Oh yes, he remembered. One day, a long time after the bombings, a lookout noticed movement some distance from the tower. At first he dismissed them for dogs. They knew about the packs of maddened beasts, had seen them many times prowling the areas close by. There were times when they assailed them, while they were busy clearing the rubble in the immediate vicinity of the building. And because of them, they had had to build a higher wall around the cemetery since the first few burials they made there did not rest in peace for long.

Ben was shocked at hearing this. His clan never buried their dead. They always burned them. Otherwise there was no telling the amount of rats and dogs that would come to feast upon the dead.

Nel went on. After some time, the movement the lookout had spotted got closer. To his amazement, he saw two people, walking together, each one carrying a large bundle upon their shoulders. They stopped for a long while to rest just beyond the clearing, giving the lookout enough time to take pictures of them. At the boy's puzzled look, Nel explained how they could use a device to take pictures of objects far away and promised to show him when possible.

For the people of the tower this was a great discovery and from that day on observation times where increased tenfold. Every minute of every hour there would be someone watching. Cameras filmed the surrounding area all day and night. After a while it became evident that the chance sighting of the two people was not accidental. During the following months and years they spotted several persons–men, women, sometimes children. They were haggard and badly dressed, but they survived against all odds. And suddenly the scientists' fire of curiosity flared anew. Who were these people and how had they survived the radiation? Had they come to seek refuge from another country, hoping to find somewhere safe to live? So many unanswered questions.

Long debates ensued. Should they try to contact those people or just observe them from afar? Should they try and infiltrate them, get to know more about how and where they lived? What were the dangers? Finally, the three leaders of the tower met and decided to form a new group whose sole purpose was to observe and study the people of the Desolation without trying to make contact.

Those were the rules, and the team obeyed.

To his great satisfaction, Nel was selected as a member of that group. Their excitement was palpable. For the first time in the history of the tower, they were going away from the tower to investigate, to walk the Desolation among the rubble and deserted streets. Not a single one of them had ever ventured farther than the cemetery. He had longed for this chance so much and finally it would be a dream come true.

Using protective gear that helped against the dangers of the radioactive environment, they found themselves patrolling the deserted streets, in search of the people they had so often spotted from high above. Readings from the equipment they took with them confirmed the readings of the equipment within the tower: it showed them that radiation levels were still high for them to be safe. This made them wonder once again whether those survivors had somehow adapted themselves to the toxic surroundings.

As he walked amongst the fallen houses, Nel often tried to imagine what a particular street had looked like before the bomb, how life must have been for the people living there. He said it was like living in one of those models for a time.

Days, weeks and months went by. Sightings were few and furtive, but the signs of a group of people living in that area were unmistakable. They found several dug up areas, tracks left in the dust by the people whom they referred to as the Survivors. Slowly, they started identifying these survivors, and soon they realised that these people lived in some sort of community. Their search parties were organised, their searches methodical. Apart from the fact that they were as thin as sticks, they looked otherwise quite healthy, which led the team to a very revealing confirmation. The survivors *did* somehow adapt to the toxic environment. This was good news indeed.

As it happened, the people they were

following were those of the Taàr. About the other community, that of the Baron, they knew nothing. It was only after Sal had captured Nel and Karl and decided to send them to the Baron that they realised there were actually two communities of survivors on the island.

As he had said before, Nel went on, their instructions were to keep a low profile and avoid contact. Until one day, the cards on the table changed completely. Something happened within the tower that would force their hand and change the history of events forever. The last girl in the tower, Ela, died while giving birth to her only son. The moment he was born, all hope of a legacy died. Their knowledge would be lost forever, locked away in the most secure building on the planet, totally inaccessible.

Russ, the boy said. Nel nodded to confirm he had guessed right.

Was it destiny or just pure chance that since the day the doors of the tower closed for the first time, no other girl except Ela was born? The few women present in the tower when the atom bombs fell grew older, mothering only boys, then died with the resentment that they could not bear a girl. He should explain at that point, Nel said, that although there were some great minds within the tower, none of them was any expert in childbirth or artificial insemination. What's more, with the tower still being incomplete, there was only a semi-functional clinic available. It was not equipped to carry out experiments on genetic modification. Ben understood nothing of this, but did not interrupt the story teller.

With that Nel stopped for a few moments, as if the memories had taken him back to other times, now long forgotten. He resumed after a while.

Those were hard times. Arguments rose inside the tower, factions formed. Some took Ela's death as a sign. The Nimbus Tower, the project design to withstand the mightiest disaster was destined to become an empty tomb where thousands of years of human knowledge were to be buried until the end of the world. In a way, it was akin to the same destiny of the great pyramids of Egypt. Did Ben know about them? When the boy gave a negative answer Nel told him there was so much to show him from the past. Many wonderful things. But not now. Another time. Now he wanted to continue this sad story.

The team that had been studying the Desolation and its survivors for the past ten years had a proposal to make. They went to the leaders and suggested that in view of the desperate situation, they should take their project to a new level–they should make contact with the Survivors and invite them in. This would ensure that knowledge was passed on to a future generation, perhaps to their own line of children if the women of the community of the Desolation gave their consent to bear them. In the Desolation, they had glimpsed hope.

Ben said nothing. Nel's storytelling had enchanted him, as bit by bit the story unfolded before him–a story he had never heard the like before. Sal's tales were different. They always left him feeling sad and resentful for having been born in that horrible world. But Nel's words carried hope, the promise for something better. Underneath that majestic oak, hands crossed, he hung on every word that came out of Nel's mouth.

It wasn't easy, Nel was saying, to convince their leaders. The proposal was democratically presented to all the residents of the tower and long months of debates followed. The tower split into two opposing factions–those in favour of the integration, and those against. Finally, a deciding vote was called. The final decision was taken in favour of making contact and trying to persuade Ben's people to join them in the tower.

It took years to get ready. Plans needed to be drawn and discussed, residential areas within the tower needed to be prepared for the influx. Security measures needed to be drafted. Then finally, the mission began. And from that point onwards, Ben knew how the story continued, since he was there when first contact was made, and he was the first to accept their invitation to join them inside the tower–of his own free will. Without knowing, he had proven that their project could be accomplished.

Taking a long deep breath, as if he had gotten rid of some immense weight, Nel stretched his arms, then looked into the boy's eyes.

"And now," he said, "I am going to tell you another story, and at the end of it, I will be asking your help."

The day they met for the first time, when the Taàr's people captured them, Nel and Karl's intention was to make some sort of contact. They were tired of waiting, and decided to cast the dice and see the outcome. In previous encounters they never succeeded to speak to any of the Survivors–they just ran away from them, disappearing from sight. So, when they chanced upon Ben's group, they plunged in upon them. They endured the beating which got them inside the Taàr's stronghold. However it became immediately clear to both men that with Sal there would be no bargaining. He was too determined, too hard headed, and the fact that he did not let even his own people speak did not auger well with their plan. They would never be given a chance to make their proposal. Sal would never agree to any terms.

This was why Nel and Karl decided to go back to Tartarys to try to talk to Sal again and put forward their proposal. They did just that, about a week after Ben found himself inside the tower–during this time he was being kept under observation in a sleeping state, until tests were carried out to determine how his body had been able to adapt to the radiation.

This time however, they did not go alone. They took others with them–a group of over two hundred tower people. They wanted to avoid being taken prisoners. Nel said that against all odds, they managed to get an audience with the Taàr inside the temple. He let them in, probably because their action took him by surprise, or maybe the reason was another one.

Ben felt confused and at the same time bewildered how nobody had told him anything about this before. But he kept silent. He felt the story was not over yet and he was curious to know not only what happened with Sal but also why Nel had said he would need his help.

He wasn't surprised when Nel declared that once more Sal refused their proposal. Sal started screaming in their faces, he wanted to throw them out of the temple. Things got hot and Nel and the others thought they had got themselves into a fight, but no one touched them. Instead Ben's people let them retreat and exit unharmed, without ever noticing that some of the tower people attached tiny devices to the inside walls of the temple on their way out. Outside it was getting dark, and by the time Nel and his people walked back to the town's border, night plunged in. They stopped there, and waited. From all around, rabid dogs barked and filled the night with terror. The special whistles kept them safe from the beasts.

The devices they attached inside the building were an invention of scientists from the past–a little box from which a potent gas was released, putting everyone who breathed it immediately to sleep. This assured that nobody would get hurt–Nel and Karl knew that the Taàr clan would all be gathered in one place at night and they used this knowledge to their favour.

Ben could not believe all this. But he still kept quiet. He heard how the tower people forced the doors with special tools, then used some kind of vehicle to transport the sleeping bodies from the town to the tower during an entire night. Once inside, they were placed in a quarantine area where they still slept under observation. Before waking them up, the doctors wanted to run all the tests to ensure no epidemic infections were introduced inside the tower.

The tests were now done and as from that day they would start reviving them. That's where Ben's help was required. If they found a friendly face upon waking up, Nel was sure their shock would be lessened. He might be able to help his friends integrate more quickly by sharing his own experience with them.

Nel stopped at that point. He had been talking for a long time, without tiring, without slowing down. Now he observed Ben's face, calculating, trying to gauge his reaction.

And Ben didn't know how he should react. When he heard how Nel and his friends 'handled' the clan people back in Tartarys, he had felt a blow in his stomach. A part of him wanted to keep on believing that Nel was a true friend, with good intentions, but another, deeper and older self, a part of him that grew inside him among the rubble heaps screamed and shouted with rage like a cornered rat. He was so absorbed trying to understand these conflicting feelings and thoughts that he didn't notice that Nel was calling his name and asking if he was alright.

Then when he finally did hear him, he turned his head and just stared into Nel's eyes, searching for an answer to the doubts that clouded his thoughts. He needed to take a decision, one that would help his friends. He felt responsible. He felt he owed them greatly. But most of all, he felt used. Enraged, disillusioned, disappointed. Guilty. That was the right time to ask his brother's advice, since he was wise in a way Ben was not. *Rorik*, he thought, *why did you leave me alone?*

Time went by. The man and the boy sat silently next to each other, in the shade of the tree. One waiting and hoping, the other looking inside himself for the best answer.

"I'll help you," he said at last.

# 9 WORDS LEFT UNSPOKEN

He lost count of the number of attempts he had made to enter the area where his friends were being kept. He felt as if he had made that same walk a thousand times in the last three days. And probably he had.

Nonetheless, Ben persisted.

He wanted to talk to Sal, but every time they stopped him, telling him he was not welcome in there, that he was a traitor and that the Taàr didn't want to see him.

Even Edgar and Dalin and the rest of the Younglings refuscd to speak to him. They stood there, a few meters from him, hands crossed, their looks sour. And after all those visits he still couldn't get used to the sight of his old friends there in front of him, dressed in new clean clothes, their faces and hands free of the grime and the dirt. Although they had been given the same clothes as those worn by the tower people, Tartarys adult males could still be easily distinguished at first glance–their beards and dark skin stood out.

But it was the girls and the women who attracted the greatest attention. And with them, the little children and the babies, some running around, some playing quietly, some shrieking as only babies can do. The whole area was ablaze.

Lost in his thoughts, Ben hurried on through the silent corridors towards the Tartarys Hall–that was how everyone in the tower now called the newly inhabited quarters. A whole floor had been dedicated to housing over four hundred new denizens, with enough rooms for everyone. However, his people preferred to group together in that immense hall. It was so huge, so vast, that with over four hundred people in it, it still looked quite empty.

At one of the entrances to the quarters, Ben was met yet again with a crowd of familiar faces that seemed to flock together just to bar his way. But this time he kept going. He pushed through the human wall, ignoring their shouts to stop and proceeded through a throng that quieted down as he passed. Angry eyes followed him but this time he took no notice. No one laid hands on him or tried to stop him. He hoped no one would. He was angry.

Ben hadn't slept since the day Nel asked him for his help. On that same day, Kim did not wake up.

Nel told him that for some unknown reason, Kim died in her state of induced sleep during the revival process. He assured him the doctors did all they could for her, but in the end they had to give up. The boy took this news badly. Sorrow gripped his heart and did not let go.

He felt guilty for Kim's death as well even though he had done nothing to bring that fate upon her. And he felt cheated by Nel and the others who had become his friends in a very short time. When he had decided to go to the tower, he had done so on his own. That was one thing he wanted Sal to understand–he had gone alone, and never spoke to anyone about his previous life. He was afraid of what the old man thought of him. Sal might assume that he had helped the tower people to capture them when he knew nothing of their plans.

As he went by, people stopped talking and just looked at him with their accusing stares. Some started shouting names at him. Traitor, they called him, and coward. They wanted him to go back from where he came.

But Ben didn't leave. He kept on walking until finally a group of man just made him stop and there was no way he could free himself and keep going, no matter how he tried. He knew he could go no further. Silently, they held him, made him powerless, accusation in their eyes. Ben realised that everyone had stopped talking and now only the children could be heard, laughing and screaming and crying.

"I want to speak to the Taàr," he told them, his voice strong. "Sal, I want to speak to you. Where are you? Listen to what I have to say," he shouted in the general direction of where he thought Sal might be hiding.

More name calling, more accusations. Until a voice echoed throughout the hall, ancient and harsh. It quieted everyone, even the young children.

The hands that held him suddenly let go. The human wall in front of Ben split to offer him a passage through. He walked in behind them and found himself standing before the back-bent figure of Sal, seated on a chair, staring down at the floor between his legs. It was not the sight he expected. Sal looked as if he had grown older instantly, as if the years that had been following him had finally caught up and surpassed the old leader.

Without moving an inch, without even looking up, the Taàr asked him if he had come to tell him he was free to go. If not, Ben might as well leave immediately.

Those words where not unexpected, but still they hit the boy like a punch to the nose. And the words left unsaid had twice the effect. Ben wanted to answer him, he wanted to tell him so many things. That he felt sorry for Kim's passing, that he had done nothing wrong, that Sal should at least listen to Nel's proposal . . . but he couldn't bring himself to speak.

So instead, he turned his back and walked slowly out of the hall.

Sal's wish was clear. He wanted to go back to the town. And if that was what he wanted, Ben felt he should do everything he could to make it happen. He felt that was the only way he could redeem himself of the guilt over Kim's death.

So he went to look for Nel.

No, Nel answered from behind the white desk where he was sitting. No, he could not. He was talking in gentle tones as if afraid he might hurt the boy, who, furious with rage, had asked his questions roughly, angrily. The gentleness had no effect on Ben. The answer was not the one he wanted.

And so came the inevitable next question.

"Why not?"

Nel moved forward slowly until both palms were face down on the polished surface of the desk while he looked straight into Ben's eyes.

Because if they let Sal go, others would leave with him, possibly all of them. After all, Sal was still their leader even inside the tower walls. And after all the work to get them inside it would be a shame to lose them in such a silly way, just because a seventy-five year old man could not grasp change.

Ben, who had remained standing in front

of Nel's desk, now grabbed a chair and set down.

"That seventy-five year old man," he said, his voice trembling with frustration, "has just lost the woman with whom he has lived since before you were born. And her death is your fault," he finished through clenched teeth, pointing a finger at the man.

Nel was so taken aback with this accusation that he recoiled back in his chair as if he had been slapped hard. His hands went through his hair while contemplating what to answer.

Letting out a deep breath he said that he knew it was his fault. That was the truth. He felt responsible and he accepted the blame. Kim was the only one to die in sleep and they had investigated the matter. They found out that Kim had a heart condition they had failed to diagnose. There was no way to make up for their mistake, because nothing they could ever do would help bring Kim back to life.

"You can let old Sal go," Ben said.

"Release him and let him go live with his sorrow in the place where he shared his life with Kim. You can help him, if you want." And not for the first time, Nel felt confused and amazed because the boy in front of him was wise beyond his years.

No. No, he could not, the man said. He could not. And there was another issue as well. How should he tell Ben? Better to go on and say it. From the medical examination they carried out on Sal, results show that he was terminally ill and should have been dead quite a long time ago. The doctors couldn't understand how he could still be breathing. They also said he could die any day.

Perhaps his decision was cruel, even inhuman, but the needs of the many outweighed the needs of the few. That was why he could not let him leave. Not at that crucial point.

Ben felt himself freezing on the chair. He understood now why Sal had shrunk so much. The old man had lost the reason and the will to live. Kim was everything to him. Now he had nothing left to fight for. Ben felt horrified that the man he had always thought to be so strong, so indestructible, was now on the point of death. The boy said nothing, but in his mind he was already making his own plans.

"And what about me?" he asked Nel. "Can I go out of the tower or am I also a prisoner here?"

Nel answered that he hoped Ben would understand that for the benefit of his companions, it would be better if no one exited the tower. He wished his friends would have the opportunity to live like the boy himself did for the last few weeks. He reminded him that he himself had remarked how Nel was right and that life inside the tower was better than in the desolation.

If the Taàr clan get used to the tower, it would benefit all parties and both their future and that of the tower people would be brighter.

There was a grain of truth in those words, like there was in Rorik's words who once again was present inside his little brother's head, giving advice from somewhere beyond death. And he was saying that there was always something hidden behind a kind gesture.

Ben knew Sal well enough to understand that once the old man had said he wanted out of that place, nothing would change his mind. Not if he had to die trying. But Ben also knew that life inside the tower was truly better than outside. He was sure that in three or four weeks time, none of his friends would opt to go back to their ruined town.

Nel was right. If the old man left now, many would want to go with him without having the opportunity to experience their new home. It was a difficult and hard decision to take for a boy his age. But he had been sleeping on hard surfaces since birth.

He got up, resting both hands on the desk and looked Nel in the eye.

"I will do as you say. On one condition–I want my friends to be happy. I will take care of the old man myself."

With that last statement, Ben turned his back on Nel and stormed out of the room. As he walked back, fists clenched and tears welling in his eyes, he felt the cold metal of the whistle he had just stolen bite into his palm.

Decisions had been made.

Sal was sitting in the same place as before, by the huge window, this time surrounded by a dozen men who stopped talking as soon as they felt Ben's presence. A reddish afternoon light cast sharp shadows on their faces, making them look grim and angry.

Ben stood there, looking at them, defiant and determined. He breathed in slowly, taking in his surroundings. The Tartarys hall was high up in the tower and the view from the window showed a good portion of the Desolation, from west to north of the entire island. Someone with good eyesight could even catch a glimpse of lands beyond the black water. A view of an open bleeding wound that brought only sorrow and sadness.

Most of the people were gathered at the back of the hall, opposite the large window. There they could look onto one of the inner terraces, enjoying the view of the lush green plants and trees, the birds and the animals, the same things that had enchanted the boy since his arrival in the tower a few weeks before. The youngest of the children from Tartarys ran after each other among the trees on the terrace outside, laughing and screaming.

But Sal being Sal would never give himself the luxury of such views. Instead, he sat as far away from the terraces as he could. His place was by the large window, his world was the Desolation. Perhaps it was the last act of resistance he could offer now that they had been captured. His one good eye, the window of his own heart, was open on what had been his entire life.

Ben thought Sal looked even older than before, even though only an hour had gone by. *Perhaps*, he thought to himself, *this is because now I know he's dying.*

Why had he come back? It was his Uncle Sam's voice that asked the question, delivered with his usual lack of grace. Ben ignored him. He went around him until he found himself once more standing in front of the Taàr. He was aware of the others around him, standing with their eyes and ears open.

"Can I speak to you alone?" he asked.

Sal turned his head and looked straight at the boy. Slowly, he gestured towards the others, signalling them to leave. They obeyed, but the look on Sam's face spoke volumes. Ben looked at him and smiled. He was rewarded with a flash of anger from his uncle.

When the others were out of earshot, Ben let out the breath he had been holding. He felt he had won the first battle of a war to come. He had planned everything carefully and that first success filled him with the courage to go on. *Now*, he thought, *for the second battle.* He weighed his words well before speaking. Sal let him take his time. *Unusual*, thought Ben. *Perhaps another sign of his illness.*

"You were right. As always," he said, smiling slightly, but the smile evaporated when the old man remained unmoved. He put on a serious face and went on. "You were right. They are not going to let anyone out of here before a number of weeks go by. Perhaps months. Their intention is to give our people enough time to get used to life inside the tower. They want them to remain living here but they would prefer if it were their own choice. In the end, what they want is that our people join theirs and our women bear their children. If they let you go, they know that most of our people will follow you."

Sal's face remained impassive and Ben felt as if the old man knew all of this already. When he made no move to speak, the boy went on.

"I can get you out. I have found a way–it

may be a little dangerous, but it is the only way. I do not think we have any other choice."

Ben kept his eyes locked on the old man. Now came the hardest part.

"I do not believe that our people should be denied this place. This is their only chance to get out of their misery, out of the hell that's out there. This tower is a piece of paradise that can offer safety to our people, and a better life. It's sad to grow up and live a life without never knowing your parents or having to live with the grief of losing your brother."

Again, Sal sat in silence, half his face awash in that odd red light reflected by the clouds. Ben thought he looked like an ancient statue, like the ones he had often seen in picture books. Slowly, Sal's head turned towards the window and for a long time he just stared at the desolation below him, with the boy standing behind him.

"When?" Sal asked after an eternity.

Ben smiled.

# 10 THE TAÀR

Hours later, on that same day, Ben made his way once more towards Tartarys hall. As he walked through the white corridors of the tower he encountered different groups of men. They were all debating the integration of his people with theirs and how it would affect the future of the tower. He listened with half a mind to many different scenarios, to problems they could face, to things that would need smoothing down. Some were still against this 'madness', others argued that finally they had been blessed by a miracle.

He listened, but was not really paying attention. His mind was elsewhere, plotting, calculating.

He found Sal waiting for him in the same chair, looking out of the same window at the same ruins. Night was fast approaching and a semi-darkness had already settled across the land below.

Silently, the old man stood up, supporting himself on a walking stick. Ben was startled. It was an image he would never have imagined of witnessing.

"We go?" he asked. "Let's get this over with."

Ben replied with a nod and together, without saying anything to the others around them, they walked slowly out of the hall. No one asked anything. No one tried to stop them. The boy took the lead as soon as they were outside–he knew the place better than Sal. He led the old man through a series of corridors until they found the lifts which took them up towards the topmost floor. Ben had been up there six or seven times with Russ since waking up inside the tower.

The lift doors opened and the old man looked around. He walked to one of the large glass doors that led onto the immense doughnut roof and stared at the dark blue sky and at the first stars that twinkled coldly in the twilight.

"So what about this plan of yours?" Sal asked, turning back towards Ben. "You want to throw me down from the roof?"

And although he kept a serious disposition, Ben was aware that the old man was trying to make a joke. The boy smiled but said nothing. Instead he went to a secluded corner from where he pulled out a black bag and then something large and long wrapped in a dark material, something he himself had hidden there earlier.

He put the bag to the side. It made a thud when he set it down on the floor. Next he opened the large bundle in the middle of the floor and started assembling a quantity of metallic tubes together. When done, he unrolled a brightly coloured piece of canvas and attached it to the metal frame he had just built. When it was done, standing there before them was a glider, just like the ones the tower people used in their races. He had managed to steal the one Russ used for training. *Perhaps, one day, I will find a way to apologise*, he thought. *Perhaps.*

Before taking the glider outside, he meticulously checked every joint and every knot to make sure the glider was set up correctly.

Slinging the black bag onto his shoulder, Ben signalled Sal to open the large doors for him so he could take the glider outside.

Up there, there was still enough light to see by, but just in case, Ben had brought his old torch with him. It was safe in his pocket.

As soon as the glider was halfway through the door, the strong wind lifted the light aircraft and almost took it away from him. Sal promptly grabbed the glider from the rear and together they managed to hold it steady.

"We need to tie ourselves in the seats," the boy shouted above the noise of the wind.

The old man laughed, and for a brief moment, Ben saw once more the Sal he knew.

"Why? So if we crash they may find what's left of us?" he asked.

This time Ben laughed. He was sure the old man was only joking. He realised that he had just discovered another side of Sal that he never knew existed.

"It's not difficult to keep the glider steady once we ride the current," he said, with the authority of someone who knows what he's talking about. "The secret is to jump correctly and then I must hold the steering bar tightly against the strong wind."

While speaking, he went through all the details Russ had mentioned whenever they spoke of the gliders. Russ had confided with him that his dream was that someday he would be able to glide down from the top of the tower. That was the source of Ben's simple plan. Silently, he thanked his little friend.

Russ had told him that the strong currents that hit the tower had an upward lift that would give a glider the push it needed to fly away from the building without risking being smashed against it. Then it was a question of riding the right current and glide slowly downwards.

Easy. At least in theory.

He looked at the clouds slightly below them and all around them.

“What I don't know is in which direction we should jump. I know only that we must go against the wind.”

“Then we should jump to the north west,” the old man said, pointing. “The wind is blowing from that direction.”

They climbed in the glider beside each other and Ben tied both their straps. Next, he opened the black sack he had kept for last and took out two helmets. He put on one himself and handed the other to Sal, who looked at it distrustfully, then donned it. It was a tight fit for him.

"Why do I need this?" the old man grumbled.

"So that when we crash and hit each other's heads we don't crack our skulls," he answered, smiling. Sal laughed.

With the heavy winds pushing them back, they stood on their legs and inched their way towards the low wide wall that surrounded the whole roof. They managed to climb onto the wall with great difficulty, since the wind kept sweeping them back.

Then they crawled to the very edge. Although it was now almost complete darkness, the bluish hue emanating from the tower walls illuminated the surrounding clouds enough to see by. It was an eerie feeling. Ben was glad that the clouds hid the view–he knew they were at an incredible height but knowing is one thing, seeing is another.

"This friend of yours, Russ, has he always

managed to make it safely to the ground?"

"Didn't I tell you?" Ben replied, "they don't fly outside because the air makes them sick."

And as soon as the words had left his mouth, he gave a strong push forwards and they went out into space. The glider caught the upward current and was lifted higher than the tower to the sound of Sal's swearing and Ben's hysterical laughter.

The currents around the building were too strong, making them zigzag this way and that. In the bluish light of the tower, the old man and the boy inside their little craft seemed like a moth circling around a bulb.

After the initial lift they began spiralling downwards with the boy finally gaining some control. He steered into the north west but a strong gust that had ricocheted off the tower hit them hard and made them loose control once more. The glider started turning in circles, round and round like a little toy top. They went through the clouds, the sudden cold dampness shocking them both. Then they were through, flying below the layer of clouds.

Their first lungful of air made them choke. Silently, Ben chided himself for forgetting to bring some sort of protection from the dust scattered by the wind. They both coughed and spat, but no one complained.

Making a huge effort, Ben managed to stop the craft from turning and pointed it back into the wind. Flying outside of the tower was a completely different experience. The wind out there was extremely strong and he had to struggle with all his might to keep the glider on a straight path.

Bit by bit they distanced themselves until at last the currents let down and the light from the tower diminished behind them. They finally found themselves flying freely in a blanket of darkness.

Ben relaxed a little now that their flight was constant, and instead focused on the next problem, something he was not keen on tackling until the right time. He needed to find a way to determine how high above the ground they were flying so that they would not risk crashing when going down. But the darkness was complete and there was no way to tell. He turned his head until his mouth was close to Sal's ear.

"Can you try and take out my torch light? In my pocket," he shouted. "When you find it, turn it on downwards at small intervals."

The old man understood the instructions. He got the torch out and shone it briefly downwards. But the light was lost beneath them. They were still too high up.

Ben manoeuvred the craft slightly down and for a long time they glided, with Sal switching the torch every now and then to check their altitude. It took a long time before the old man declared that he had finally spotted something. At that point, the boy asked the old man to keep the light on and together they searched the ground beneath them for some familiar landmark. Sal asked Ben to steer to their left, and for some time they kept that direction.

"We're getting close now," Sal shouted.

"Hold tight, I'll try to land," Ben replied.

He tried to slow their momentum but something came out of the darkness directly in front of them and they hit it hard. The glider turned on itself, then upside down, and they crashed hard into the ruins of some large building. They rolled and tumbled for a long distance until the glider stopped suddenly against a huge boulder.

It was some time later when the boy and the old man regained consciousness. A blanket of darkness was still wrapped around them. They lay there in a tangle of bent metal and shredded canvas.

Ben tried to move but a sharp pain in his left shoulder made him stop. He had dislocated his arm. Slowly, he tried to move his legs. They were both bruised and he could feel his pants sticking to the wounds. Using his good hand, he took the torch, still strapped to the old man's hand and pointed it towards his companion.

Sal had hit his head against a rock with such force that the helmet broke. Blood trickled from the side of his head onto his face. The eye patch was gone and Ben nearly felt sick when he looked into the empty eye socket in the fading light of the torch.

The Taàr was breathing heavily. His good eye squinted in the light.

"Where do you think we are?" Ben asked.

Sal took the torch back from the boy, re-charged it until the light it gave became stronger, then showed it around them. After a few moments he seemed satisfied.

"We're close to Tartarys. Come, let's go," Sal said, with renewed enthusiasm.

They helped each other get out of the wreckage, then started walking towards the direction indicated by Sal. But after a while strength seemed to fail the old man as the adrenalin wore off. He started faltering, his breath became ragged, and the boy had to step in beside him and help him along using his good arm.

"I'm as good as that walking stick of yours," the boy said, smiling in the darkness.

Sal laughed but said nothing and they fell silent. They walked along, unspeaking, one not accepting the fact that strength was failing him and that he needed to be supported, the other finding it hard to understand how a man as strong as Sal could be reduced to that pitiful state so quickly. They walked on, in total silence, until Sal spoke. Three words that cut the darkness like a cold sharp blade.

"I'm dying Ben."

And the boy, with tears at the edge of his eyes, replied with just two words.

They kept on walking.

Ben was tired. More than tired. He felt exhausted and knew that if he stopped he wouldn't be able to start walking again. Hours had passed since their crash landing. Hours during which he had half carried Sal along the dark silent roads. And minute after minute, the old man had leant more and more on him. Ben *felt* him getting older as time went by.

In the past hour, the old man had started talking to himself and shaking as if he had some kind of fever. At first his words were incomprehensible, but after a while, the boy realised that Sal was reciting a list of names. A long, long list, calling name after name, ones he didn't know, others he did. Vance, Dan, Arian, Alain, Nick, Marias, Jon, Evan, Drey, Kim, Bert, Mora, Resa, Natan, Jan, Mona, Mike, Stan, Laine, Enne, Dwan, Ren, Rorik . . .

The list went on and on and only after recognising his mother's, father's and brother's names did he start to understand. Those were real names, the names of people who were once members of his same clan. People who had long since passed away into the longest and darkest night. People for whom Sal felt responsible. Like a father.

Ben didn't comment or try to engage the Taàr in conversation, but listened in silence to the old man's reverie, concentrating on his voice. It helped him ignore the fatigue and continue the slow walk towards their final destination.

At one point, dogs sprang out of nowhere and encircled them, barking and growling, barring teeth that glowed white in the artificial light of the torch. Ben reacted quickly. Using his free hand, the one he had dislocated, he painfully brought out the whistle he had stolen from Nel and blew it.

As if by magic, the dogs dispersed immediately, whining, with their tails between their legs. They went on. And after a while the sky changed its colour. A new day was dawning.

Oblivious to everything, the old man kept on reciting his list of names. He hadn't even stopped when the dogs came. But as soon as the boy mentioned that they had finally arrived in Tartarys, Sal stopped as if snapping out of a trance.

They walked into the town through familiar streets, the wind whispering around the usual total silence. After more than six weeks in the tower, the boy had gotten used to the screeching and the singing of the birds. When he compared these two opposites, he could define the silence of the town as a sign of decay and death, while the loud noises in the tower represented life. He missed the birds. He longed for their sweet, sweet song.

But there were no birds there.

They stopped in front of the temple.

Although Sal never told him where he intended to go, Ben knew how special that place was for the old man. He knew that if a place existed where the Taàr would want to while away his last hours in the world, that would be the place. The filtered light of the sun illuminated the east in a reddish glow. They looked at it for a moment or two, then together, they walked inside.

Sal removed the boy's hand from under his arm and went forward alone. He dragged his feet along the dull marble floor until he was standing at the centre of the temple, just below the broken cupola from where a reddish light came in, tainting the walls and the faded paintings. He stood, alone, without any aid, hunched under an invisible weight that had invaded his life so quickly, making the hours they had walked through the desolation seem like years.

He cleared his throat.

"Come. Come here Ben. Come get this old twig a chair."

His voice was very dry and it echoed in the emptiness of that place. It was the first time Ben had seen the temple entirely empty.

He got him a chair from the left aisle. Sal sat down immediately, with a sigh of relief. A sigh that seemed to confirm his plan eventually did fall through and he had achieved his aim. He sat and seemed at peace all of a sudden. Then, he started talking.

"Did I ever tell you that this place, our home, used to be called a church? That was the name of this temple. And it was a centre of activity for the whole town. People lived in the surrounding houses and they would come here every single day, to pray to their god, to worship the figure of a naked bleeding man nailed to a wooden cross. They believed in pain and suffering, the ones who came before us. They believed that redemption came from misery. And history has proven them right. When man forgets what his ancestors suffered, he starts scheming a new way to annihilate himself. I'm sure that someday he will be successful."

Sal turned his good eye towards the boy.

"Remember, you must never forget, suffering is what unites us and what makes us strong. Remember your roots, the ones you have grown here in this derelict town."

Sal stopped for a moment, breathing fast and shallow breaths. During this pause he opened the shirt the tower people had donned him with. From around his neck he removed the heavy golden chain with the cross attached to it and motioned the boy to go closer.

"This is for you. It's yours now. You are now the Taàr. Take it, wear it around your neck and go. Go back. The others need you, they need direction and someone to remind them of how long they suffered, of the loved ones we lost, of the times we went to sleep hungry and thirsty.

"Go, leave me alone. I am the past, you are now the future."

Stunned and unbelieving, Ben reached out and took the golden chain from the old man's hand.

For a very long moment, he just stared at the cross dangling from it.

He was going to protest, to refuse the offer. He wanted to ask Sal if this was some sort of joke. But when he looked into that old eye he knew it was not and solemnly put it round his neck.

Then, for one last time, Ben looked into the old man's eye, turned his back, and went back to the tower.

# EPILOGUE – IN THE PLACE WHERE HE FELT FREE

A silence louder than any scream fell inside Tartarys hall as soon as he set foot in it. All eyes turned on him, some with hatred, some with curiosity, some questioning, but all of them accusing. They had found him guilty without giving him the opportunity to defend himself.

All the way from Tartarys to the tower he had pondered on what he would say, on what words to use to convince his clan of Sal's will. He didn't believe that he could be successful, not when he himself did not believe this was real. How could they take him seriously? Every time he tried to visualize himself, entering and delivering his speech, he saw the scornful stares, the laughs to his face. And yet, the part of him that never let go screamed at him that this would be his biggest challenge. Only if he succeeded in this would he be worthy of leadership. He knew that many would not be willing to accept him. So he tried to imagine their arguments and created counter arguments in his mind.

He assumed that those closest to Sal would pretend the leadership of the clan and contest it, fighting. He was sure about it. So why had the old man chosen him as his successor? Why had he picked *him* from among four hundred and fifty people, one of the youngest in the clan? What had he seen in him that he hadn't found in the others? In Uncle Sam for instance, who not only shared Sal's same hard and determined nature but was also close to the old man, possibly one of his best friends.

He had planned every word, every reaction. But now, those stares swept all confidence from him. The speech and arguments he had recited evaporated and left him blank. The silence grew uncomfortable until someone behind him spoke and broke the spell. He had lost his big chance of taking everyone by surprise.

"Where is Sal? What did you do to him?" Jimi asked. He was a short stocky man, his face covered in a black beard that punctuated his large eyes. He was one of the men always hovering around the Taàr.

"He's gone."

Ben's words were dry and they echoed in the hall even though he did not shout. To many there, they sounded like thunder. He felt he should say something else.

"I set him free. I went with him back to our town, and left him there to rest, as was his wish."

"You killed him!" someone shouted from the back and many took up the shout until an entire chorus of accusations was being directed at the boy.

Ben felt a strange calmness come over him. The voices rang in his ears and he focused on the sound. He was the Taàr now, he made them sing. With a gesture of his good hand he silenced them.

"You are wrong. Sal was sick, a terminal illness that came quickly. He knew he was dying and went back to die. I had to carry him the last few miles because fever took him. He started calling the names of dead people, members of our clan who died in the past."

"Liar! Murderer! You're just making this up. Sal is not there," Jimi said. The chorus took voice again, this time calling him a liar.

He knew then that words would never be enough. So he opened the tattered shirt he was wearing and took out the chain Sal had given him. He held it high for everyone to see.

"Sal gave me this. He appointed me the new Taàr—"

He did not go any further. Those words

sparked the hatred of the crowd around him. He saw them closing in on him, fists raised, rage in their eyes. He could do nothing except stand there and let them come. He felt his end was near.

"STOP!" someone shouted. "I said STOP you fools." It was a strong voice, a familiar voice. A voice he never would have expected to hear in such a moment.

"Stop. The boy speaks the truth," Sam said. He had come forward and put himself in front of his nephew.

"Move aside Sam. You don't know what you're saying," someone told him. And someone else accused Sam he was defending the boy just because he was his sister's son. They asked him to move aside, to let them teach a lesson to a liar and a murderer.

But Sam didn't move an inch.

"True, he is my blood. And all of you know that I could never stand him. But the truth is the truth. He does not lie and I have proof." From inside his shirt, Sam fished out a bunch of small folded papers. He opened these and showed them to those in front of him so they could see the handwriting on the five sheets of small paper.

Someone asked what they were, and why was he showing them those papers.

"Sal gave me this letter before he left yesterday. He asked me to open it only at dawn if he didn't come back by that time." Sam paused and showed the papers again to those around him so they could recognise Sal's handwriting. Many of them could not read, so he turned the pages back and started reading.

*"Sam, my friend,*

*If you're reading this letter, it means I'm no longer inside the tower. With Ben's help, I'm going to try and escape. He can help me–probably he's the only one who can given his familiarity with this place and with its inhabitants. Perhaps you are asking why am I leaving. The reasons are many. I hope that at the end of this letter I will have explained myself to you and to all the others who's first thought will be that I have abandoned you. Let me try to explain why I wanted to go alone.*

*There is no other way to say this, so here it is, plain and simple–I am dying. I feel death coming at me so strongly as if it was my own shadow getting longer at sundown, when there was still a sun in the sky. And my sun should have gone down long ago. Now I know that the only reason I'm still alive was Kim. I confess that I still cannot accept that she passed away. Not in that way, I can't. It's cruel not being able to say goodbye. Being separated from her weighs on my soul and on my every thought. Separation is too damn hard.*

*I have done my time as leader of the clan and now my place is elsewhere. I can feel it in my heart and in my every bone. Looking back, I believe that, with the invaluable help of people like you and a handful of others whom I could trust, I did my best to lead. Like those before me, I carried the burden with responsibility in the best interests of our people. We have faced some rough times but together we managed to pull through. But now I must pass on the sceptre of command to someone I feel is better suited for what lies ahead. Someone with a fresh mind is needed to give our people the future they deserve. To preserve.*

*Take no offence my good friend. No one needs to take any offence. I'm doing this in the best interests of our clan, of my clan, and I selected my successor without any prejudice. With this letter, I, Sal the Taàr, in my full mental faculties, name Ben, your nephew, as my successor. Perhaps as you're reading this you're wondering if it's insanity that has gripped me. I assure you, my ailment is not in my brain.*

*In Ben I foresee a great leader, something which is not evident right now. In him I see my younger self all those years ago, but I also see something I could never be. I see a future man that can bring change to our people.*

*I implore you to forget all your grudges, to put aside your personal issues with the boy–I told you this several times, the boy never had anything to do with the death of your sister or her husband, and neither with that of Rorik's. Your attitude is your way of protecting yourself from grief, from the pain the deaths of your loved ones has caused you. But distancing yourself from him is not the way. You must now more than ever reconcile with the boy. He needs you. He needs your experience and advice. I hope that you can look at this objectively and see that the boy can make it, he can lead, but only if you back him up. With you at his side, he can bring the change that is needed.*

*I know what you're thinking. No fourteen year old boy should ever carry such a burden. But Ben is tough. He has your blood after all. He will be able to carry the burden. He has proven himself to me on many occasions. But you must be there, at his side, to guide him, to offer your advice. I'm not saying this will be easy–it will not. But if nothing else, we have learnt that nothing in this life is easy.*

*I have a confession to make. To you, and to all my people. I have been hard headed. I let fear blind me. I have judged without first looking for the truth. Since those two tower men visited our temple I have been reluctant to hear any arguments that involved them and their kind. I even forbid anyone to speak of them. But since waking up from that drug induced sleep, since losing my beloved Kim and feeling the end approaching me, I have come to see things differently.*

*Can a man change so drastically, so quickly? I did not think so before, but I do now.*

*Life inside this bloody tower is so much better than the one we led just a few weeks ago. In Tartarys we lived day by day. We could not plan ahead, we could not think of a future. But here, here finally I see an opportunity. All will depend on how well we can integrate with the tower people. Ben knows this, he was the one who started it all, and he can see clearly. Every side will benefit from this union. Who knows, perhaps in a distant future, the cities will be rebuilt from today's ashes, the fields will yield crops again and trees flourish as they once did before the bombs destroyed life and hope alike. Once, when I was younger, my dream was to be able to unite all the survivors on this island, and work together to clean away the rubble to give ourselves another chance.*

*But let's not jump so far ahead. In truth, my dream died the day Kim did not wake up. And now, dear friend, my time has come to join her wherever she is. I cannot die here, not in all this comfort. I was raised in hardship and suffering, and I want to go away in the same way. I can never come to terms with luxury and comfort. I do not want to understand them or embrace them. No. I must leave, back to the place where I lived my entire life, surrounded by dead gods, grief and long forgotten monuments. There I will die in peace, there I will be free.*

*Farewell. I wish health and a long life to you and all our kin. May the future prove me right.*

*Sal the Taàr*"

## A NEW BEGINNING

# ACKNOWLEDGMENTS

Nicholas Aquilina, Karen Bonello, Duncan Caruana, Daniel Creus, Derek Fenech, Tricia Fenech Fabri, Mark-Anthony Fenech, Chris Gruppetta, Matthew Paul, Simon Prime, Chris Scicluna.

## BOOKS BY THE SAME AUTHOR

*Il-Logħba tal-Allat* (The Game of the Gods, a trilogy)
i. It-Tielet Qamar (2008)
ii. L-Aħħar Ħolma (2010)
iii. Is-Sitt Aħwa (2012)

*Unus Mundus*
i. Fil-Mergħat tal-Impossibbli (2013)
ii. Jien, Wieħed Minnhom (2015)

*Irvin Vella, Virtual Investigator*
i. Il-Każ Manduca (2015), The Manduca Case (2017)
ii. Il-Każ tas-Serqiet Strambi (2016)
iii. Il-Każ tal-Gżejjer tat-Teżor (2018)

*Dystopia*
i. It-Taàr (2017)

## ABOUT THE AUTHOR

John A. Bonello is the author of the fantasy trilogy for young adults *Il-Logħba tal-Allat* (The Game of the Gods), the duology for adults *Unus Mundus* and the series of detective novels for children *Irvin Vella, Virtual Investigator.* He won the Malta National Book Award four times. He lives in his grandfather's house, in the remote village of Dingli, on the island of Malta.